Robert Williams grew up in Clitheroe, Lancashire, and currently lives in Manchester. He worked in a secondary-school library before working as a bookseller with Waterstone's. He has written and released music under the name *The Library Trust*.

In 2007, National Book Tokens created the Not-Yet-Published Prize to celebrate their 75th anniversary. Open exclusively to booksellers, it was a one-off award dedicated to the wealth of passion in UK and Irish bookselling. Robert Williams won the prize with *Luke and Jon*, his first novel.

Praise for *Luke and John:*

'Robert Williams's *Luke and John* is told with an outsider's eye: cool and clear, and hiding deep emotion behind a carapace of coping . . . the language with which he recounts this tale of friendship and survival seems newly minted.' *Financial Times*

'It's a hell of a thing to accuse a new writer of wisdom, but that's exactly what Robert Williams's first novel has. I'd predict great things for him, but I think they've already begun.' Francis Spufford

Luke and Jon

ROBERT WILLIAMS

faber and faber

First published in 2010
by Faber and Faber Ltd
Bloomsbury House
74–77 Great Russell Street
London WC1B 3DA
This edition first published in 2011

Typeset by RefineCatch Limited, Bungay, Suffolk
Printed in England by CPI Bookmarque, Croyden

A CIP record for this book
is available from the British Library

ISBN 978-0-571-27488-8

2 4 6 8 10 9 7 5 3 1

For Kate

On a Hill

I have green eyes. Probably not the green you are thinking of now. They are bright green. They are startling. This is not a boast. I am just trying to be accurate. Precise and clear. If I told you my eyes were green and left it at that you may picture them as a shade of hazel, or olive. They are vivid green. I will be honest from the start.

When people meet me for the first time, there is often a moment of shock, a pause, and then they scramble to recover. We continue as normal. Later, the shy or polite ones will risk a quick sideways glance. The confident or rude ones will stare. They are both just checking that they aren't mistaken, it isn't a trick of the light and those really are my eyes.

I live in a house on top of Bowland Fell. The house looks down on a small town called Duerdale. I moved here with my dad some time ago. My old life finished somewhere else and my new one was supposed to start here. We ended up in Duerdale for different reasons, the practical reason being we could afford the house. We could afford the house because it's falling down. There are holes in the roof, cracks in the walls, and the window frames are rotten. 'Cosmetic problems,' my dad muttered, 'we'll take it.' He shook hands with the estate agent and walked away. The estate agent laughed and then smiled. He thought my dad was daft. My dad isn't daft. We needed somewhere to live and this is what we could afford.

He makes children's toys, my dad. Out of wood. Children don't want wooden toys. They want better phones, clothes and cash. Thankfully, some parents are stupid or old-fashioned enough to buy my dad's toys. That's why we can afford any kind of home at all. The kid gets a wooden toy and has a sulk; I get a house that's falling down.

Just to be clear. His toys are brilliant. He has won awards from the . . . wait for it . . . The Traditional Toy Makers Association. He is a bit of a hero to them. And a bit of an outlaw. He hasn't paid his subscription for eleven years but they still keep him on their books. He's that good.

I don't make things out of wood but I do paint. People say I'm very good. Sometimes they ask me how I do it, and I don't know what to say. It's easy. A lot of things that come easily to most people, I can't do at all. I can't catch, I can't sing, maths, I'm rubbish at computer games. Paint, though, makes sense to me. I know how to control it. It does what I expect it to do; it behaves for me. A teacher at my old school joked that it was a combination of having my dad's hands and magic eyes. He laughed, but it made sense to me.

There are a few standard toys my dad makes and sells at market stalls around the county – cars, boats, planes, trains, he knocks these out in his sleep. They are his stock in trade and he just bangs them out. His real joy though is a commission, the chance to make a one-off. Something special. He guarantees he will never make another toy like it again. He talks about 'mass production' and 'globalisation'. He says it controls our lives and ruins our town centres: 'Everywhere looks the same from Inverness to Ipswich.' He says people should want difference; they should want something unique, something special. And sometimes they do; sometimes the phone rings.

He will listen intently, make notes, nod a lot, and gently guide the customer in the right direction with a few suggestions. 'Beech is nice, yes, but have you thought of rosewood? Rosewood would be perfect.' He will go to his workroom and become obsessed with the piece. He will spend hours over tiny details. He will make sure joints open and close smoothly and silently. He will check and double check that everything is completely and exactly in proportion. He will sand, paint and varnish so it all looks as perfect as it could possibly look. He will then charge about half of what he should ask for. Another reason, I suppose, why we live in a house that's falling down.

This is us then. The toy maker and the boy with bright green eyes. The two weirdos on the hill.

April 11th, 4.27 p.m.

We came to Duerdale after Mum was killed. She was killed on a bright April afternoon when her small red car and a lorry smashed into each other. April the 11th, 4.27 p.m. 'It was immediate, she wouldn't have felt a thing,' they told my dad. A cliché, but it was important. She just went. In a second. Her last words to me were,

'I'll pick you up' and she blew me a kiss. I was glad for that. One boy in our class, Michael, his dad had died. They were supposed to be going to watch a football match but his dad rang from work and said he couldn't go; he wasn't feeling well. Michael didn't believe him because he'd been working so hard lately. He thought it was an excuse and they had an argument. Michael shouted at him and slammed the phone down. That was the last time they spoke. His dad had a stroke and died that night.

I found out later that they closed the bypass for eight hours while they measured tyre marks and took photographs of what was left of the car. There were tailbacks for miles across the county. They said at the inquiry that neither vehicle had any defects and both were in a roadworthy condition. The lorry had been serviced and checked the week before. It passed. They said it was nobody's fault. It was 'a tragic accident that led to loss of life'. Of course, the lorry and the driver escaped pretty much unscathed. With the size of the thing I reckon he could have driven into the moon and the moon would have come off worse. It was just my mum's car that was squashed and twisted and left looking like a piece of modern art. I saw a photograph of the lorry driver, Brian Stuart, in the local paper. It was taken at the inquiry, after he had been told he was blameless. He was dead-eyed. He looked like a ghost.

My mum was coming to pick me up from the after-school art club when it happened. When she didn't turn up I set off walking. It was the kind of spring day that tricks you into thinking that it would be summer the

4

next day and it was almost warm; car windows were wound down and shirtsleeves rolled up. I walked past traffic jams and frustrated people in cars calling home to say they would be late; there had been an accident. By the time I got home I think I was the last person in town to know. The police had been and gone. There was just my dad, sat in his chair, slack-faced.

The next morning I didn't know what to do so I did what I always did, I went to school. I walked into the classroom for registration and Mrs Calvert's eyes filled with tears. She dragged me out of the room, shoved me in her car and drove me home. She told me to only come back when I felt better. It seemed unlikely that I would ever feel better so I went back the next day. My friends and teachers all treated me differently for a few weeks. Concerned looks and gentle voices. Quiet chats in empty classrooms. They asked how I was coping, 'How's your dad?' I shrugged and muttered. After a few weeks they stopped asking. They didn't forget, but I learnt that life doesn't stop for everybody just because yours does.

My dad didn't do anything for weeks. He sat in his chair. He didn't sleep, he didn't shave, he lost weight. I would hear him at strange hours of the night going downstairs to drink. And sob. Eventually red bills started arriving and the phone started ringing. He didn't read the bills and he didn't answer the phone. My dad was never good with the day-to-day stuff at the best of times. He wasn't going to start now.

I painted more. I painted because it made my mind blank. It was like falling asleep. Falling asleep without having to dream about my mum. I painted for hours. When I painted I was empty. It helped.

A big grin

They met at sixth-form college. Mum said she loved him because he was the most unconventional man she had ever known. At first she thought he had an act. She thought he'd noticed the way all the boys tried to attract girls, and his plan was to stand out by doing the opposite. She laughed at her young self: 'I kept waiting for him to start shouting, running, pushing and flirting, but he never did. He would just let the school day pass him by, the chaos and noise, the fights and the tears. He would always be working on a sculpture or something or other. He was on a different planet. I would leave at the end of the day and he would be there waiting for me at the gates with his latest piece of art and a big grin.'

They got married the day after their A-level results came out. Some people thought it was a mistake; they should travel and see the world, see what opportunities were out there for them. They went to Loch Ness for their honeymoon, a week in a cottage on the shore. When the holiday was over they went to live back with their parents. At the end of the summer my dad enrolled on an advanced City and Guilds course in Design and Craft and my mum got a job with a solicitor in the town. They started renting a little terraced house near the middle of town and a year later I was born.

They were stupidly happy. Even as a kid I could see

that. Sometimes though, she wanted to kill him. She would go to work in the morning and ask him to make sure he posted the cheque for the phone bill or the gas, whatever. Just one thing. She would kiss him goodbye in his workroom and he would already have forgotten. When she came in eight hours later and tired, he would still be at his desk, chiselling and sanding – the cheque on the kitchen table where she left it. It drove her mad. She would shout and he would slam his workroom door and we wouldn't see him all night. The next day though, he would do the shopping, get the tea ready and there would be flowers on the table. Everything would be back to normal. It worked well when I was a bit older. I could post things on the way to school or go to the shop and buy bread and milk. He could just concentrate on his work and making me and mum laugh. We were a good team.

Melanin

My parents took me to the doctor's when I was twelve months old. They thought there might be something wrong with my eyes because they had become so bright. They thought I might have some kind of infection or sight problem. The doctor agreed and he sent me to a specialist. Apparently the specialist thought my eyes were brilliant. My mum told me, 'He kept shining his torch, peering and laughing. He did the eye tests they had for babies and said your sight was fine. He said you were very lucky to have such beautiful eyes.'

My parents were told that it was the amount of a

pigment called melanin, which determines eye colour. When a baby is born there is virtually no melanin present but this gradually develops over the first twelve months. Varying amounts of melanin or pigmentation can create different shades of colours. They were told that it was possible that as I got older my eye colour may change, the tone may calm down, but it never did.

When I was young I never even thought about my eyes and nor did any of my friends, things like that don't bother kids. When I was bit older though and people commented and I'd learnt how to be shy, I wished they weren't so unusual. Now though, they are just my eyes. Just part of me. They don't make me any more or less of anything.

Brian Stuart

Brian Stuart drove the lorry that crushed my mum's car. Did I hate him? Yes, I did. And then the inquiry said he was blameless. And I saw that photograph of him in the local paper. He didn't look like he had got away with anything. He didn't seem relieved or pleased or vindicated. He looked like it hurt him to be here, like he was thinking about what had happened every second.

The paper said which lorry firm he worked for and one day, a week after the inquiry, I went to their depot. I wanted to see him, to watch him. I stood across the road from the depot, at the bus stop, pretending to wait for a bus. I saw him almost straight away. He was sat in a Portakabin speaking on the radio. I watched him for a few days and saw that he would spray the lorries down when they came back at the end of a shift. He seemed very quiet. There was a lot of shouting from driver to driver but he never raised his voice. He didn't join in. I never saw him speak more than a few words to anyone and I never saw him drive. He moved slowly, like his bones hurt, like he had flu. Quite a few times when I went down after school he wouldn't be there at all. Sometimes I wouldn't see him for days in a row. Then he would come back, even thinner and slower than before.

I stopped going after he saw me. One of the drivers had pulled into the yard and walked across to him in his Portakabin and they spoke briefly. They both looked out from the dusty window across at me. The driver left and walked to the depot and Brian Stuart carried on looking out of the window. After a few minutes he walked out through the door, into the middle of the huge yard and stopped. He stood with his arms at his side and tears running down his face. We looked at each other and he shook his head. I think I nodded. I was crying too. A bus pulled up and I got on. I didn't know where I was going but I didn't know what else to do. I didn't go back after that.

When I found out he had killed himself, I cried. I was shocked but not surprised. He looked like he had to get out of his body, if that makes sense, like it hurt him too much to be here any more. He looked like my dad and that scared me senseless.

It was a bright morning when the men arrived with a van to take everything away. It felt like a good day for a fresh start. They were nice guys really; they seemed embarrassed by it all. I think they probably knew. Small towns. My dad made them a cup of tea as they loaded up. They cracked a few jokes and everyone laughed a bit too loud. They were pleased we didn't try to fight them or stop them or cry. We just watched. They said we were dream clients. They wished us luck, pulled down the shutter of the full van and drove off. They didn't touch my room though and they left my dad his chair and tools. Like I said, they were nice guys. Just doing a job.

The next morning Dad got up early, washed and shaved and cleaned his teeth. He still looked awful, but he'd tried. He came into my bedroom and sat next to me on my bed and hugged me. For ages. It was the first time since I walked past the traffic jams and saw him in the chair that I didn't feel like I was on the edge of the world about to fall off. He talked to me about our situation. He hadn't paid the mortgage and bills for months. We had been in trouble before Mum died but since then it had, he paused, 'escalated'. He said that things would be changing and he was sorry.

The bank took the house back and sold it to reclaim their money. My dad got a letter explaining it all and a small payment when everything was finalised. He looked at the cheque and laughed. He asked me if I would prefer 'coast or country'. We went to the estate agent and Dad gave details of our situation. They talked figures. The estate agent straightened his tie and said, 'Not around here, not even with the market as it is now.' He spoke about other areas that were more affordable, up-and-coming towns that offered good properties at more realistic prices. He made some phone calls, listened and nodded, hung up and looked at us. 'Duerdale?' he said.

We would have to move away. It meant a new school, a new town, new everything. It didn't matter. I don't think either of us cared that much. Dad did have friends but he wouldn't see them. Some still persevered but they weren't rewarded with much. People looked at him and beneath the cocked head of concern I knew they were thinking, 'Time to pick up the pieces, time to move on, no more wallowing.' I think my dad felt like I did. There were no pieces to pick up. We left the next week.

Duerdale

Duerdale: It's about an hour away, to the north-west. It's tucked between hills and moors, almost hidden, like a mole tucked between rolls of skin. I had never heard of it. Nobody I knew had heard of it. When we went to sign for the house the estate agent told us, 'Make sure you have provisions. It was cut off for three days when the last snow fell. When the rain finally washed the snow away they found two old people dead in their beds in one house.' My dad looked up at him, then back at the contract, and signed.

It was raining and windy the day we moved. It was one of those dark days that never quite fully emerge from night. The journey took nearly two hours, an hour longer than it should have done. Dad wouldn't drive on the bypass or busy roads and he drove slowly. Tense and edgy, hunched over the steering wheel. We spent most of the journey in silence. The rain fell hard and the windscreen wipers squeaked and wobbled with little effect and I watched the rain hit the road and bounce back up. We eventually reached the outskirts of Duerdale, but our house was on the far side and we had to drive through the early-evening deserted streets. It isn't the best time to judge a town – a dark day, black and raining. I tried not to shiver as we passed the unfamiliar houses and shops. It looked like a town from an old black-and-white film where the characters hardly speak and the wind bangs the gate open and closed in the night. I concentrated on the road ahead. As if reading my mind, Dad said, 'It will look better with the morning sun on it.' He didn't sound convinced. We reached the far end of town and the foot of Bowland Fell. We braced ourselves for the climb and the car strained against the gradient and the buffeting wind.

We passed a few houses and farms lower down the fell. They looked in better repair if no more welcoming than our house. Although it was only early evening, most already had their curtains drawn, closed to the incoming night. The trees at the side of the road grew thicker the further we travelled up the climb. They branched over the road from either side and embraced each other in the middle and it felt like driving through a tunnel. We turned off the main road and onto the uneven track that led to our house. The trees were gone and we had fields on both sides. The rain attacked us from all directions. We were jostled and bounced in our seats as the car lurched over the pits and holes of the track.

My dad was leaning forward in his seat, a concentrated frown on his face. The rain had started coming down harder and faster, like lines of thin steel from the sky to the ground. Tiredness hit me from nowhere. I slumped. I felt Dad turn to me, a glance to see if I was OK. I was about to return the look with a smile. I didn't. Just as my head turned, out of the corner of my eye, I saw a shadow appear in the road. I shouted. The car screeched and tensed and slid to the left. Stones from the track jumped into the air. We scrambled to a halt.

Standing in front of us, *inches* in front of us, was a boy. Dripping wet, mouth open. It was hard to tell through the dark and the rain, but he looked a couple of years younger than me. He stood with his arms at his side, white skin, glassy-eyed and no expression. Mouth open. He looked at me for a second, turned his head and looked at my dad. Then he was gone. Running hard and fast across the fields and disappearing through the pouring rain. We watched him go. 'Jesus,' my dad said, 'we nearly killed our first local.' He was sweating. We sat there for a couple of minutes. He laughed nervously, trying to lose the shock. He put the car back in gear and we set off, even slower than before.

We drove for a few more minutes, rounded the final

bend and I could see the house, silhouetted against the hillside. I tried not to focus on it too much. We pulled to a stop and stayed sat in the car, unsure of the next move. Dad sighed and roused himself and I followed slowly. We climbed out of the car, he unlocked the front door and we stepped into the house as the new owners.

This is my house

I remember the print-out we had been given the first time we came to view:

Some structural work needed. Good opportunity for renovation. Interiors need updating. An ideal chance to buy a detached country property at a realistic price.

It was a hole. We had been told that the previous owners, the Thornbers, had lived there all their lives. They owned the land around the house and it had been a working farm. For the last fifteen years though Mr and Mrs Thornber had just lived in the house and rented the land. They refused help from the council and refused to move, even when they found it hard to get about. I thought about how grim it must have been stuck on top of a hill, unable to move, hanging onto each other and seeing out their last days. Waiting to die. From the state of the house it looked like they spent the last few years living in one room and I found out later that they were the couple who died together in bed when Duerdale was cut off. It didn't bother me much to be honest. I don't believe in ghosts. I quite liked Mr and Mrs Thornber. If you are going to die, die in old age in your own bed with your lifelong partner. Good for them, the stubborn old sods. Their house stank though – it really did.

Nobody had bothered to clear out any junk. The estate agent probably assumed whoever bought the house would knock it down and start again. So we were left with the Thornbers' heavy, dark furniture and collected junk. I should have been grateful; we didn't have any junk of our own. It didn't feel like a home. Most of the floors were just wooden boards, but not like the floorboards a lot of my friends had in their houses. These were dirty and rough and uneven; you couldn't walk barefoot. The walls were painted a dismal grey and the curtains were thin and stained and none of them fitted properly. In some rooms they were pinned to the window frame so you couldn't even open them. There were odd chairs and pieces of furniture scattered around. Everything mismatched.

I lay in bed on the first night. The rain battered the walls and the wind chased itself through the holes and into and around the house. The windows rattled and shook as the wind rushed them. I was worried I would wake up on a pile of rubble looking up at the stars. I hadn't thought of the boy in the road since we got to the house; we had been too busy. But as sleep started to come, I saw him again. Standing in front of the head-lights, straight-armed and open-mouthed in the pouring rain. I tried to work out why he looked so unusual. In the last seconds, before tiredness finally covered and carried me away, I realised – he was dressed like my granddad in his old school photos. My sleepy mind tried to claw itself back to the surface, to think some more, but it was too late. I had already surrendered. I was asleep dreaming of storms, strange-looking boys and car crashes.

Primary colours

My mum was fun. She was bright. She was clever but I don't mean bright like that. She was sparky.

When I was a little kid and I got picked up from school she was always easy to spot amongst the crowd. In the winter I just looked for her red hat, bobbing amongst all the other heads. A traffic-light red. In the summer it would be her daisy hat. Her toenails and fingernails changed colour at least once a week. She'd ask me, 'Iguana green or orange?' Sometimes she would alternate, one toe orange, one lizard green. For special occasions she had nail varnish with glitter in it. My dad had made a cabinet just to hold all her little bottles of varnish. She added the fairy lights.

She had a huge collection of ear-rings, bracelets, necklaces and bangles. None of them were expensive. She picked them up at market stalls, craft fairs and charity shops. She sometimes made her own. Her ear-rings were her favourite. Some of them were daft to be honest. There were massive hoops, bright-pink flowers, yellow suns. She even had a pair of snow-globe ear-rings she wore every Christmas Day. My friends loved her. She was a lot younger than a lot of other mums and it showed. She talked about music and TV and stuff like that to them. Sometimes I had to drag them away.

I will tell the truth. It wasn't always like that. She would be bright, bright as she ever got and then suddenly there would be a crash and tears. Dad would say, 'Your mum's tired, let's give her a rest, eh?' There would be no ear-rings and no coloured nails. Lines on her forehead and thinner lips. She would be in bed. Dad wouldn't be in his workroom as much and we would have Chinese or chips from the takeaway. I wouldn't really see her. Then after a few days I would come downstairs in the morning and she would be sat at the kitchen table, hugging a cup of tea. Ear-rings, bracelets and bright nails. She would pay me too much attention, grab and tickle me. She was back.

It's not what I asked for

The first morning in the new house was uncomfortable. I felt self-conscious, like the first day with a new haircut. We ate breakfast, stiff and still, like we were strangers in a hotel. Dad tried to brush the atmosphere away: 'We'll paint your room first and sort out the spare room. You can use that for your painting. Loads of natural light – it'll be perfect. I'll have the outhouse as my workroom. We'll be straight in no time . . .' He was sat in his dressing-gown, thin and tired, staring ahead. Dark eyes and stubble like passing clouds in front of his face. I nodded. He was trying hard. I looked around the kitchen at the jumble of chairs and the stained table, at the damp patches on the far wall, the pile of junk in the corner and the filthy windows. I smiled at Dad and tried not to think about the old house and our old life.

He collected the bowls and cups off the table and said, 'When we have the house sorted out a little we'll go into town, get our bearings, find out where the shops are and get your new blazer.' A small shiver ran across my back. With everything that had happened the thought of starting a new school had been buried at the back of my head, deep down. Suddenly it rose up for a second and I was surprised to discover that I even cared. I think Dad noticed me tense, he didn't say any more, just rested his hand on my head as he left the room.

My old school was OK. First I went to the primary school at the end of our road and made friends there. When it was time to move to the high school we all went to the same one – there was only one in town. Before the summer holidays we had a practice day. We all left the primary school together and met the children from the other schools. There was an assembly, we met our form teacher and found out where our classrooms were. I even knew some of the kids from other schools already from around town, from friends of my parents. It was bigger and noisier, but I got used to it. I settled straight away.

There were loud kids, quiet kids, funny kids, stupid kids, leaders and geeks. There were the sporty ones, the clever ones and the useless ones. I wasn't one of the popular kids but I wasn't with the nerds either. I was the art-room kid. It didn't matter that I didn't have the best clothes or that I had strange eyes or that my dad didn't do a job like the other lads' dads. I was OK. I was accepted I suppose. I had a few friends and we were mainly left alone. I spent most of my time in the art room and that was accepted. That was my role.

I even started getting a bit of interest off some of the girls. Shy looks and giggles, that kind of thing. My mate, Ian, told me they thought I was mysterious. He told me that girls loved artists, 'They think they're mysterious . . . you think you could teach me a bit of drawing?' He slapped me on my back and laughed.

I was glad it was the summer holidays, but I knew that as far away as the school term seemed now, it would come and one day I would be climbing into a different uniform and walking down strange crowded corridors and I would be the new boy with the dead mum. But what worried me most was having to start again. Everything was settled at my old school. It wasn't always brilliant but I knew who to avoid and who to trust. I knew my way around. This would be a new school in a strange town and everyone would be established. I would have to start again, earn my position from scratch and I didn't know if I had the energy. I didn't know if I cared enough any more. But still, every now and again for the rest of the day, a cold sliver of fear shot through my stomach.

We settled into some sort of routine for the rest of the week. I would help Dad in the morning as we half-heartedly painted, scrubbed and chucked out junk. It didn't seem to make any difference to our tumbledown house though; however much we cleaned and tidied it looked a wreck. After lunch I would help for another hour and then dad would send me off. 'Watch TV– do something kids are supposed to do.' He needed to drink and brood. I chose to paint. A pile of rocks and stones.

Painting rocks

Our house was almost at the top of Bowland Fell, but not quite. There was one more rise. I could leave our back door with my art stuff strapped to my back and push up over the final climb. It was a steep climb, but worth the effort; at the top I looked down onto the roof of our house, and further down onto Duerdale. It was an impressive view of tight streets, low houses and dark mills. The blackness of the buildings settled like a scar on the floor of the valley. To the left of the town stood the local cement factory, grey quarries, like giant moon craters spreading out behind two tall chimneys.

The rocks were in a pile at the very top of the fell, marking the summit. It was the colours that first attracted me. I didn't realise how many different colours you could have in stone. There were shades of brown, green, grey, black, even faint reds and blues if you looked carefully enough. They felt as different as they looked. Some stones were as smooth and round as marbles and had soft patches of moss you could use as a pillow. Others were coarse and pitted with edges that could rip your skin. There was a lot of different texture. 'Texture is vital' – the wisdom of my dad. He could tell a type of wood purely by feel. He told me it was important to think about the material I was painting. To consider how the object felt to touch and to try and convey that onto the paper. He said I should use all my senses to paint, not just sight. I was learning what he meant and painting the rocks and stones was good practice. I set up each afternoon at around the same time, but always in a different place. A pile of rocks and stones sounds static, I know, but these really weren't. The light changed hour by hour and the stones changed colour. Shadows came and went and the stones seemed to shrink and grow.

I paint quickly. I started and finished a painting in an afternoon. The finished paintings were lined up against a wall in my bedroom. My dad didn't normally go in my bedroom but I caught him looking at them. There were three so far. He stood for a long time. Considering. He told me they were good. He meant it. My mum said all my paintings were brilliant and she meant it too, but Dad could tell the really good ones. I'd decided to paint one each day for as long as I stayed interested. It kept me busy. It kept me blank.

A hug on a hill

It was a Wednesday afternoon. I'd set up with my back to the house. I looked up at the sky to see what kind of light I had. It was a low, liquid grey sky and you couldn't see the sun, but I knew it was behind the cloud; I was squinting and when I looked back down at my paper dots of colour flickered and darted across the page. I blinked them away. I looked at the stones for the first time and saw the envelope. It was unavoidable. I paused, brush in mid-air.

The envelope had been pushed into the pile, wedged between two stones. I had to edge it out carefully so it wouldn't rip. I prised it out safely and turned it over. My name was written on the front, in black ink: *Luke Redridge*. The writing was thin and shaky, like a seismograph had spelt it out in a force eight earthquake. I looked around quickly, to see if I was being watched. I was stood alone on top of a hill and felt like a licked finger in a cold wind. I didn't see anybody. I opened the envelope and turned the paper written side up and read.

Death is nothing at all
I have only slipped away into the next room
I am I and you are you
Whatever we were to each other
That we still are
Call me by my old familiar name
Speak to me in the easy way you always used
Put no difference in your tone
Wear no forced air of solemnity or sorrow
Laugh as we always laughed
At the little jokes we always enjoyed together
Play, smile, think of me, pray for me
Let my name be ever the household word
    that it always was
Let it be spoken without effort
Without the ghost of a shadow in it
Life means all that it ever meant
It is the same as it ever was

There is absolute unbroken continuity
What is death but a negligible accident?
Why should I be out of mind
Because I am out of sight?
I am waiting for you for an interval
Somewhere very near
Just around the corner
All is well.

I felt sick. And dizzy. The ground lurched up to me and fell away in a second. I stuffed the paper back in the envelope and shoved it deep into my pocket. I grabbed my paints and paper, strode down the fell and into the house. I slammed the back door shut and went straight to my room and climbed into bed. I slept through until the next day.

Funeral

I remember the details more than anything. The sound of the funeral car's tyres on the road as it slid to a stop to pick us up. The small puddles in the pits and hollows of the church's cracked old pavement. I was surprised to see how they had almost dried up by the time we came back outside, how bright and warm the sun had become. I remember feeling shocked when my gran hugged me. She was wearing the perfume she always wore to church and that didn't seem right. I remember everyone standing for a hymn, the silent pause, the organist's arm mid-air before the hymn started and the breath-filled second before everyone started to sing.

The church itself seemed different. I had been there many times before: christenings, weddings and harvest festivals. It was quieter today. It felt more useful somehow. Like it was fulfilling a purpose. I'm sure nobody checked a watch, nobody's thoughts wandered and nobody thought about what they had to do later. Everyone was focused.

The eulogy and the hymns, the big stuff I suppose, I'm not sure I took those in. I remember a line or a phrase. 'A much loved wife and mother and daughter, taken from us too early.' That came through. I watched dust particles drift through the air and felt like my body wasn't mine any more.

I remember what my mum said: 'I wouldn't want to be buried, stuck in a wooden box with worms eating my eyes. Burn me up! Turn me into ash and throw me into the sea. We'll all be thrown into the sea when we're dead and then one day, sometime, somewhere, before the earth dies we'll all be swept together again as we pass each other on different tides.'

She laughed and me and Dad laughed with her. She would know she was sounding a little manic, but it was only a little and she could be like this for weeks before it got worse, and sometimes it never did. Sometimes she was just exuberant.

My mum loved the sea. She told me that two-thirds of the planet is under the sea. 'Think about it Luke, think about all the places man hasn't discovered on earth and then think what must be down there. There are mountains and deep, deep hidden seabeds no human eye will ever see. There are continents of undiscovered land under water. Vast areas of blackness, beautiful creatures and secrets we will never know. That's where I want to end up.'

So we didn't have to bury her. It made me think: Why would anyone lower the body of a loved one into the cold ground? Throw some mud on them and let them slowly rot? I don't believe in God and heaven and hell but I did care what happened to her and I much preferred the thought of her remains being at sea. Being tossed and turned in a wild black storm at three o'clock in the morning or being sunned and rocked gently on a calm afternoon. That seemed more like my mum.

Afterwards everyone spoke about how busy it had been. There wasn't enough room on the pews, people had to stand at the back. I wasn't aware of that. My grandparents had taken charge – my dad's parents. Me and dad were ushered into the car, into the church, up to the front pew and then back out into the bright sun. We didn't have to do anything. People came across to us, shook our hands, kissed us, hugged us, offered condolences. We nodded and let them do what they had to do.

Everyone was invited back to my grandparents' house. Dad and me went too but after a few minutes he took me by the shoulders and steered me out of the hushed house. We went home. Our house was empty and silent. My dad sat in his chair to drink and I went to my room and sat down and had the thought: What are you supposed to do on the afternoon of the day you've cremated your mum?

The first time I met Jon Mansfield was 7.30 on a Thursday morning. It was the day after I'd found the envelope tucked into the rocks and I'd been asleep for fourteen hours. I didn't hear the knocking on the front door but I did hear my dad yelling up the stairs. Eventually. I think they probably heard on the other side of the fell. He was shouting that I had a visitor, that I should get out of my pit. I was too tired to be confused by the fact that someone was here to see me in a town where I hadn't met a soul.

I stumbled down the stairs and remembered the note from the day before. The memory was a punch in the stomach and I wanted to go back to bed, to give up on the day already, but I felt the fresh air rushing up the stairs to greet me and I knew someone was waiting. I reached the door and Dad stepped aside and my eyes met the bright morning. I blinked and squinted and saw that I was facing the boy in the road for a second time. Even in the early-morning sunshine he looked unusual. He had on the same granddad clothes: brown shoes, grey trousers and a dark-green knitted jumper. He was even wearing a bloody tie. He had a side parting that revealed a thin white line of scalp on the left-hand side of his head and each strand of hair looked separate and solid like it was being held in place by glue. He looked like it was 1945 and he was on his way to church. My dad had left us to it and we just stood looking at each other. For a long time. I squinted at him and didn't know what to do. He had a coughing fit. He recovered himself. Eventually he spoke. 'Your eyes are very green. Emerald green. Did you get my note?'

I was angry first. When I read it – stood out in the wind, high on the hill – it felt like a message from my mum, a hug I never expected to feel again. Then I'd shaken sense into myself. It wasn't from my mum. She was dead. I didn't think she was just around the corner. I didn't think she was watching me. I thought she was killed in a massive car crash and we turned her into ash eight days later. I felt stupid. And it was this boy's fault. Standing outside our crumbling, shit, house at 7.31 in the morning in stupid clothes with a stupid haircut. 'That was you.' He nodded that it was. I turned and walked down the hall and into the kitchen and dropped myself into one of the Thornbers' old chairs. I felt exhausted. I felt like I could sleep another fourteen hours straight.

He'd followed and sat down at the other side of the kitchen table. Neither of us spoke. His right leg tapped and his neck twitched and he stared at the kitchen wall like there was something there that only he could see. He coughed a dry hard cough every few seconds, his skinny chest nearly jumping out of his jumper like it was trying to escape. I'm not sure he could even tell that I was annoyed with him, that I wanted him out of the house. I thought he might be retarded. Eventually, he started talking. He spoke quickly, in machine-gun rounds. Leg still tapping, neck still twitching.

His name was Jon Mansfield and he went to Duerdale High School. The head of year told them that I would be starting next term and she'd told them about my mum. She wanted everyone to be 'supportive and welcoming in a difficult time'. He said he knew it was me when we nearly killed him, that nobody moves to Duerdale, most people try to leave, so it had to be me. He lived in a house further down the fell with his grandparents and had seen me painting on the top of the hill. He pushed the envelope into the rocks for me to find. He thought it would be a supportive and welcoming thing to do. He told me that the passage was written by Canon Henry Scott-Holland. That he had been a canon of Christ Church Oxford and he'd formed the Christian Social Union. He said that it's one of the most popular readings at funerals. 'I thought you might like it – someone gave it to me when my mum died.' He came to a halt, he was finished. He'd tried to be kind, so I tried to swallow my anger, looked at the strange creature sat opposite and asked if he wanted a cup of tea.

He just started showing up

The rest of the summer holidays began to follow a pattern. Dad let Jon in every morning at around 7.30 and shouted me out of sleep. I stumbled down the stairs and into the kitchen and into a chair opposite an already seated Jon. I would be a bit useless for the first few minutes as I tried to shake my head awake and steer my thoughts from dreams back to reality. Even before my mum died I'd had horrible nightmares that hung around the corners of my mind for hours, colouring the whole day. My currrent nightmares involved a lion, loose in the house, hunting me, eating and clawing its way through doors. It always ended the same way: paws on my chest, mane tickling my face, teeth bearing down. Even in daylight the memory made me shiver. Dad would put the kettle on and disappear to his workroom and I would make me and Jon a cup of tea and after what could be a few seconds or a few minutes, Jon would start talking. As he spoke I watched him, his twitches and tics, his jerks and shudders. He was like a small, wild animal. One at the bottom of the food pile with the most predators, never relaxing, sleeping with an eye open. His eyes constantly darted around the room and he was always tapping one part of his body against another. He was thirteen like me but looked at least two years younger. He only stood as high as my shoulder and his tiny wrist looked like it would snap with the weight of lifting the cup of tea from the table to his mouth.

It was one of the first mornings Jon visited and I was stood by the kettle, squeezing a tea bag against the side of a cup and watching the water turn dead-leaf brown. I was still half asleep and only half listening to him rattle on. He was telling me that he lived with his grandparents. That they don't have a TV and have lived in the same house all their lives. They used to be friends with Mr and Mrs Thornber, he said, but they fell out in a dispute over who owned a corner of a field. He told me that they don't like strangers or incomers. I couldn't help thinking as I passed him his tea that they sounded like a pair of miserable bastards. He took the cup and put it down on the table, blew on it and said, 'My mum died when I was six but I remember loads about her. I never met my dad. Do you know about Duerdale?'

I told him I didn't and tried to concentrate as he reeled off the facts.

'It's an old mill town, situated in the base of the Bowland Valley. Most of the houses are terraced houses, back to back, set out in grid form . . .'

I sipped from my tea and he told me that the cotton-mill owners built the houses and that when you started working at one of the mills you would be given a terraced house to live in. He said that all the houses are very close to the mills so that the workers didn't have far to go, but it was also so the mill owner could keep an eye on his workers. They were built during the Industrial Revolution, he said, at the end of the eighteenth century and the beginning of the nineteenth century, and in a lot of places they've been knocked down because they aren't considered suitable for modern living. He said in some towns they knocked down terraced houses and put up flats instead and moved everyone from the houses to the flats. He looked amazed as he considered this and said wasn't it ridiculous. I'd never thought about it and I didn't care but I nodded that it was anyway.

He looked up at the ceiling, rocked his head from left to right and carried on. 'We live on Bowland Fell which has mainly been used for sheep and dairy farming in the past but there aren't as many farms now because of foot and mouth and supermarkets.'

He came to a halt. He'd finished. I passed him the biscuit tin, but he'd already stood up. He walked out of the kitchen, down the hallway and the front door banged closed behind him. The tea sat on the table, still steaming, untouched. I considered him for a moment. He was weird. Mum would have liked him.

Whisky in the Jar

It took me a while to notice how bad it had become. I don't think either of us saw each other clearly for a few months. And it wasn't easy to tell what the grief was responsible for and what to blame the drink for. They seemed inseparable to me. I only know which came first.

He'd lost more weight. I saw bones in his face I'd never seen before. Everything about him was harder, sharper and smaller. He looked like he'd almost halved in size and now his beard seemed too big for his face, like it had started to take over. He wore the same clothes most days: a pair of old blue jeans with holes that were eating the rest of the material and a dirty green jumper. I shouldn't say but he smelt. We communicated in grunts and nods and shakes of the head most of the time but every few days he would react like he'd remembered something important. His head would shoot up, or he would spin around quickly and ask me something like, 'Have you got your lunch money?' or 'Have you cleaned your teeth?' I would nod and he would look relieved and say, 'Good . . . good.' He didn't clean his though. I touched his toothbrush each morning as I cleaned mine and it was always dry.

I don't remember when I started noticing but it got to be that there was always a glass of whisky in his right hand. He held it low and to his side, almost behind his back, so that maybe I wouldn't notice. When Mum was alive he used to buy bottles of beer, different brews with silly names, 'Blond Witch' or 'Bowden's Bathwater', but he never came back with those now, just the whisky.

He didn't neglect me. He always made sure there was food. He would ask what I wanted from the supermarket and I tried to be sensible. I asked for stuff I knew Mum approved of: carrots, peas, lettuce, leeks. It's just that chips are easier. We didn't eat together. I never really saw him eat much at all – a bite of bread or a handful of cereal. He did sit with me while I ate though: two fingers of whisky to my fish fingers and chips.

It wasn't like I was invisible, he was trying, I could *see* him trying. See him mustering the effort from somewhere. He would shake himself together when I walked in the room and I would watch him try to pull all the threads together and attempt to focus. I could see him try and quell the steel splitting headache and swallow the queasiness away. He would lift his head and peer through the fog and try to arrange a smile. He still hugged me sometimes. It was great. Even with the smell. I don't know how often he made it upstairs to bed. He never made the bed so it was hard to tell if it had been slept in. I saw him a few times, late at night, asleep at the kitchen table with a drop of whisky left at the bottom of the glass and his head on the table.

He was still always up before me, no matter how bad he looked. He would be sat in his chair at the kitchen table with the morning sun streaking through the greasy windows, spotlighting his grey face and bloodshot eyes. His shaky hands were always wrapped around a cup of thick black coffee and if his hands were trembling too much he would leave the room and come back a couple of minutes later, less jumpy. I knew he went for a drink and he must have known that, but neither of us let on. He didn't want me to see him drinking too early that was all.

Panthers and Pluto

It turns out that Jon wasn't retarded. He was massively strange but not even slightly stupid. He knew facts about things I didn't know existed. He spent a lot of time at Duerdale Library and had his own corner there. He didn't read any fiction though; it was all cold hard fact. He could usually be found upstairs in the reference room, with the encyclopedias and dictionaries piled high around him. He had a photographic memory and if he read about something it stuck. It wasn't a magic power or anything; he just remembered things. And I enjoyed testing him. Our early-morning meetings would consist of me throwing random words at him: 'electricity', 'Jupiter', 'Islam'. Occasionally he wouldn't have read about one of the subjects, so I would try another word and off he would go. He wasn't showing off, it was just how we began to communicate. Early-morning lessons in whatever.

It was a good way for me to begin the day, it would slowly clear my mind of the dreams and nightmares. I would wake up over a cup of tea, and listen to Jon chatter about the different types of eagles found in north-west Scotland, their wing spans, colouring and diet. He would explain why Pluto is no longer considered a planet: 'It's too small, it doesn't dominate the neighbourhood around its orbit so it's called a dwarf planet now. They've given it the number 134340. Some astronomers cried when it lost its official planet status.' He would tell me that a wild panther can run at 35 mph and can be seven feet long from nose to tip of tail: 'If it stood on its hind legs it would be taller than your dad.' His eyes were wide as he considered this fact. He looked across at me to see if this information had really sunk in. I nodded quickly, to show him I was impressed too.

I would occasionally ask him about school or friends or his grandparents but he never said much and just kept on tapping his leg. So I would throw another subject at him, take a sip of my tea and watch him go.

His silence about school frustrated me. I wanted to know about Duerdale High, what to expect, what the teachers were like. When we went to buy the uniform my dad asked if I was nervous and I shrugged and told him I wasn't bothered, and part of me really wasn't. But occasionally, at unguarded moments, I would be hit with a slice of fear. In the middle of a painting or just before falling asleep the unease would shoot through my belly or skate across my spine. My mum always told me to confront my fears. She said that things are rarely as bad as your imagination makes them. So I tried with Jon again.

'Jon, what's Duerdale High like?'

Silence.

'Jon, what are the teachers like?'

Silence, leg starts tapping.

'Jon, what are the other kids like?'

Silence and leg tapping and neck twitching.

He looked uncomfortable and I felt mean. I let it go.

Dad and Jon

He seemed to like Jon. I think he saw, like I did, that Jon was the kind of stray my mum was drawn to. She was always on the side of the dismissed or the fragile. When we went to choose a cat from the RSPCA she chose the oldest, and scruffiest, the one that no one else wanted. She even asked which cat had been there the longest. Me and Dad laughed when they showed us. He was an old, ugly, ginger tabby that spat and snarled when you went near. One ear half bitten off and a mean face. My mum insisted we would have him. She said that he spat and snarled because he had to spit and snarl to survive, that he just needed somebody to care for him. She was kind of right; he eventually stopped scratching. He would find my mum as soon as she walked through the door and fall asleep on her all the time. We called him Rasputin. He never liked me and Dad though.

Anyway, we were the kind of family that welcomed . . . outsiders, I suppose. Having Jon around made us both make more of an effort. One thing we were never allowed to be when Mum was alive was rude. Rudeness and dropping litter were up there with grievous bodily harm in her book. With Jon in the house my dad had to speak now and again. Or at least grunt.

Jon was fascinated with my dad's toys. I remember his face the first time he walked in the workroom. He looked like he had woken up on the moon. His eyes were popping, big and wide, and his mouth dropped open and didn't close all the time he was in there. He walked the perimeter and let his arm reach out and hang over all the toys. He didn't touch any of them, his left hand just hovered above cars, soldiers, trains and boats, following their contours, shapes and lines. After his first visit he was hooked. He started going there every day.

The workroom was an outbuilding, just a few steps from the back door. It must have been used for cattle when the house was a working farm and there was still a warm animal smell sometimes, just for a few seconds. On a couple of his better days my dad had whitewashed the inside walls and fitted work surfaces. It was just like his room at our old house except much bigger. On three of the surfaces were rows of toys he was making, each row at the same stage of completion. He did each step for each range of toys at the same time, so all morning he would be painting all the car bodies red or sanding all the feet of the soldiers. It saved time and made sense but sometimes he joked that it was like working in a factory. The fourth work surface was empty. At our old house he used this for his wood carvings and sculptures. He laughed when he called it 'my creative space' but I knew he meant it. It was the desk where he enjoyed the work the most. It was where he made the stuff he wanted to make, the pieces that never sold at the markets because they were too expensive or too weird, or both. The fourth desk was still empty here though. There were no strange and ugly carvings of bizarre, angry creatures or giant men, carved out of wood and painted steel silver.

I didn't know how my dad would react to Jon's presence. He wasn't used to having someone with him when he worked and me and Mum had always just left him to get on with it. If the door was closed, he was working. Maybe Jon disarmed him, like he had me. After a couple of days, I dared to look in, to see what was going on. I saw my dad showing Jon some simple techniques: sanding, cutting and shaping.

There were quite a few breakages, snapped pieces of wood and cut fingers and blisters, but then, after a few days, it seemed to click. There wasn't the usual Jon chatter. He was quiet and concentrating and it was the only time I saw him relax. His eyes stopped darting, his shoulders dropped and he was absorbed. And he was good, it came as easily to him as painting came to me. Within a few days he was attempting the racing cars that my dad made and I wondered how such an awkward body could produce such smooth and controlled pieces. I watched them one afternoon and they seemed happy in their silence, hunched over their wood, sanding and shaping. I didn't feel left out. I went to paint my rocks and stones on the fell and at the end of the afternoon we would meet up back in the kitchen. Me with paint-flecked hands, them with wood shavings in their hair.

A lot of things I took for granted were new to Jon and I was almost jealous; it was like every day was Christmas Day for him. I remember the night we got fish and chips. It was a Saturday and Dad had been selling toys at a market all day. He'd had a good day and sold loads of stock and on the way back he stopped off at the chippy. He'd bought three lots knowing that Jon was most likely round. We sat down and Dad passed out the three warm bundles and the tangy scent of warm, salty chips and vinegar filled the room. We didn't bother with plates or knives and forks; Dad just dumped some kitchen roll in the middle of the table and we got stuck in. Jon seemed unsure what to do. He watched Dad and me unwrap our food and start scooping it into our mouths. Dad looked across the table at Jon sitting watchful and silent. He nodded towards Jon's food and told him to go ahead. Jon unfolded the bundle like he was opening a present and might want to use the paper again. Still looking unsure, he selected a chip, held it in front of him, looked it over suspiciously and sniffed it before putting it in his mouth. He chewed slowly, paused, chewed a bit more and swallowed, and smiled. He selected another one and this one went down a bit faster. Eventually he picked up speed and there was less selection and hesitation and more chewing and swallowing. We all finished and sat there for a while, full and fat and satisfied. After a couple of minutes Dad started to grab all the paper together, as he leant across Jon to get his rubbish he asked, 'Good?' Jon nodded firmly, and said, 'Yeah, it was, thanks.' He was as sure as I'd seen him.

He didn't take to everything as easily. Whenever he was around and I put the TV on I could see his restlessness increase. He would normally last about five minutes before he wandered off. It was the opposite with his books: put one of those in front of him and he was transformed, shovelling the information from the page into his brain and filing it away. I made the mistake of trying to play a computer game with him once. He was useless, worse than me, even worse than Dad. I tried to be patient and showed him the buttons to press to do the moves he would need. And I put it on the easiest setting, but I could have beaten him blindfolded. It wasn't any fun and I could see he wasn't enjoying it so I turned the screen off and we didn't play again. He was quite happy reading a book or messing around in the workroom as my dad got on with his carving. When he turned up at our door early in the morning I was pleased to see him. He was absorbed seamlessly into the daily routine and he fitted well. It was good to have him around. It seemed to me that two people alone in a house sometimes don't have to see each other all day. They can follow different routes to different rooms at different times and schedules need never overlap. But with a third person to-ing and fro-ing there is a bit more rhythm somehow, a bit more connection, and a bit more life.

I dreamt about you last night
and fell out of bed twice

I found a small piece of map in the car the other day –
'Cleobury Mortimer', wherever that is – and laughed at
a memory of her for the first time since she died. I know
where the ripped piece came from; it was from when we
went on holiday a year ago and we were in the car and
lost and had been lost for a long time. I was sat in the
back and I could feel the tension pouring off both of
them. I tried to ignore it and kept my head down trying
to duck under the argument-ready air. Dad kept glancing at the unfolded map sitting lazily on Mum's knee
and eventually snapped. He couldn't hold it in any
more. He shouted: she had the map and it was her job
to direct, he had to concentrate on the driving. She
could at least open the thing and make an effort. All she
had to do was one bloody thing and she wasn't bloody
doing it. Typical. He finished. Silenced exploded in the
car and he was already looking sorry for what he'd said.
He stole a glance to see Mum's reaction. She had been
expecting the blame, I could tell, but not at this force or
this volume. She looked straight ahead, hands resting
on her knees. She was assessing the situation and planning her retaliation. After a few seconds she'd decided
her move and acted. She lifted the map up in front of
her, made a show of slowly unfolding it, and held it out
wide between her hands like she was holding up a bed
sheet. She tore it right down the middle and then ripped
neatly and tidily until the map was a pile of tiny pieces.
She gathered them together into one fist, taking her

time, and then threw them into the back of the car. Dad's gaze had been quickly alternating between the contours of the unknown road and Mum's tearing hands. I could see that he wanted to protest, to tell her to stop, but somehow the words didn't come. There was furious silence for about half a minute until Dad found his voice again and told her that now she was just being a bloody lunatic, we were in a strange part of the country without a map. Bloody brilliant. Bloody well done. I thought the shouting was really going to get going now and braced myself but before he got to the end of the sentence he started laughing. Mum sat with her arms crossed, staring straight ahead as he laughed and spluttered and apologised and tried to kiss her cheek and still drive the car along an unknown road. He had to cajole her for ages before she forgave him. She made him accept full responsibility for being lost and made him buy us an ice-cream each. Not for him, just me and her. She wasn't really mad any more now either, it was just pretend mad, but she kept it up for a while anyway, so Dad knew that he was still on probation. He didn't care, he was just happy to be forgiven. For months afterwards, even after Dad had cleaned out the car, we would still find tiny pieces of ripped map, stuck between seats or in corners of footwells. Mum said that we should have saved each piece as we found them and made a new road map of the United Kingdom and Dad said, after she'd left the room, that the way she read maps it probably wouldn't make any difference.

I saved the piece of map in the back of my wallet. It was good to remember her and I thought about her all the time. I was scared I would forget what she looked like, how she moved and spoke and smelt. Sometimes it felt like her face was disappearing from my memory, like the images of her I held in my head were dissolving. To try and counter this I looked at photographs of her, but she was one of those people who look different in almost every picture ever taken and none of them were quite how I remembered her anyway.

The dreams of her though, they were the opposite; they were too real I suppose. They were worse than the nightmares and almost stopped me going to bed. When I was awake I missed her badly and it hurt, of course it did, but at least I knew the truth. The dreams muddled everything up. They gave me her back for a few minutes. My normal dreams have always been silly, colourful and weird, just like everyone's dreams. I remember when I was a little kid and I dreamt that the school had been taken over by bright-red robots. We tried to fight them but we couldn't win and someone said that it was pointless, a waste of time, so we made friends with them instead. Some of the robots became teachers and some of the smaller ones were pupils like the rest of us. I can still see it now; it's stayed with me all these years. When I got older I would sometimes dream I was being chased down black streets by wild dogs and men with guns or that I was naked on the school playing field, desperately trying to hide from pointing fingers and laughing faces. I would toss and turn myself awake and after a second relief would flood through me and I would find a cool patch of pillow and fall back into sleep.

When I dreamt about Mum it was different. It would

be simple everyday things. We would be walking through town on a Saturday morning, on our way to the butcher's, or we would be in the supermarket and I would try and sneak more chocolate into the trolley and she would catch me and make me put it back on the shelf. Every last dull detail, every sound rang true, everything exactly as it was a few months before. That's what made the mornings so horrible. If anyone ever invented a drug where you dreamt like that without ever having to wake up, it would sell faster than chocolate, heroin or booze.

Are you ready?

It was a Wednesday in the middle of the summer holidays when I decided to go and see Jon. He had stopped visiting us. He'd been strange for a few days, even twitchier than usual. He'd spoken less and stayed for a shorter amount of time. Even my dad had noticed. 'Do you think Jon is all right?' he asked. I shrugged, 'It's hard to tell.' He nodded and went to his workroom. I did miss him though. The days dragged without his chatter. He broke the static and silence.

I was bored and a bit concerned. But mainly bored. And starting to get jumpy about school. It wasn't too far off now and I needed to occupy myself. If Jon could just turn up here first thing every morning without an invite, surely I could visit him. He lived in the next house down the fell and I could just about see it through the trees from my bedroom window. It wouldn't take long.

It did take long. I fell in a stream, I got stung by nettles and I ripped my trousers and skin on a rusty old nail as I climbed over a fence. And it was as hot as hell. I sweated into every corner of my clothes and my throat was as dry as the Atacama Desert, which is in Chile and, Jon told me, is the driest desert in the world. And when I rounded the final corner it looked like it had been a waste of time. The house standing in front of me looked like a ruin. Even compared to our ruin. The windows were cracked and loose and covered by yellowing newspapers on the inside and the roof looked about ready to avalanche its way into the front garden. I would have to fight through the undergrowth to get to the front door and there were tractor tyres and rusty engine parts scattered everywhere, like traps set to snap at ankles. Nobody lived here surely? I was about to turn away and reluctantly push my way back up the hill when I noticed the smoke, slowly spiralling out of the shaky-looking chimney. Somebody had a fire going on a hot morning in August. Somebody was home.

Dry heave

I can't forget the smell. It still hits me sometimes. Like it's stuck in my nostrils.

I clambered through the garden, wrestling with trees and bushes, easing my way past rusty obstacles. I pushed through the final overhanging branches and almost fell into the front door. With a sense of victory I knocked and waited but nobody came. I knocked again, a bit louder, hoping the decrepit door would withstand the contact and the vibrations wouldn't shake any roof slates into a slide but there was still no response. I pushed my way round to the back of the house and tried again on the back door. There was no sound of feet approaching, no sound of anyone being home at all. I looked up again to check that I hadn't imagined the smoke, and sure enough there it was, still lazily drifting out of the chimney and out into the hot fell air.

Eventually, reluctantly, I gave up. I resigned myself to the long hot climb, and started to force my way back through the tangle of shrubbery. Halfway down the path, just as I was negotiating my way past a vicious-looking exhaust pipe, I heard the front door pull open. I got my balance and turned to see a worried Jon peering out from behind the door. He saw it was me and his shoulders dropped a little. I smiled. I shouted, 'Are you all right?'

'Yeah.'

'Can I come in?'

'I don't know.'

I laughed. 'Why not?'

He looked unsure but then he waved me back towards the house.

He pulled the door back a couple of inches and I asked what the problem was.

'They don't like visitors . . . they don't like strangers.'

'Well, I'm not a stranger, am I? And I'm dying for a drink, I think I'm about to pass out.'

'OK, but I'll have to show you to them, they heard you knocking.'

He pulled the door back further so I could just about squeeze in and I pushed myself through the gap. Jon closed the door behind and we were engulfed in darkness. My eyes adjusted and I could that see we were in a cluttered, dirty hallway. We were stood very close; there was nowhere else to stand, junk piled everywhere. I could feel his breath on my neck as we stood still behind the closed door. And then I was hit by the smell. It was like the house had taken a deep breath and exhaled. It stank. A mixture of mould and damp and decay. I covered my nose and started to breathe through my mouth. Jon gave me a second to compose myself, pushed past me and led me halfway down the hall and through a door on the left.

I followed him into the room and nearly fell over a heap of newspapers. They weren't just covering the windows, they were piled high in paper mountains throughout the room and scattered across the floor. Most had turned yellow but some were new: fresh white backgrounds with inky black print. The room was bursting with headlines: 'Violent Crime Doubles'; 'Street Knife Attack Terror'; 'Karaoke Granddad Wins Top Prize'. And then I saw the cats. They glared at me and scurried into corners. I could see at least four straight away and it smelt like there must be more and it smelt like they used the room as a toilet.

It was a few seconds before I noticed the reason Jon had brought me into the room in the first place and I hope I didn't gasp when I clocked them sat there but I can't be sure that I didn't. Just below my eyeline, right in the middle of the room, sat two small old people.

Hunched over in chairs, dressed in bedclothes, with bright eyes, clear and staring. Jon coughed and shuffled his feet and said, 'These are my grandparents.'

Upchuck

They didn't speak. They just stared. White hands riddled with green and blue veins and blotched with dark spots gripped their chair arms. Their skin looked like cheap tissue paper, like it would dissolve in the rain. Jon's grandma rocked backwards and forwards in her seat like she was trying to push her chair closer to me. His granddad held his chin high in the air and to the left, keeping his fierce watery gaze trained on me. Either he nodded at me or his old head wobbled of its own accord. I couldn't be sure and I didn't want to stare, so I offered a quick nod in his direction. I didn't really want to look at either of them at all so I ended up looking at my feet. I hadn't done that for years. Nobody spoke. A confident cat rubbed up against the back of my legs and I wanted to run. Jon wasn't any help; he remained silent and I had no idea what to do. Thankfully, eventually, Jon started to walk out of the room and I followed, closer than his shadow. We turned left and walked further down the hallway, stepping over piles of clothes and rubbish and through into the kitchen. Plates were piled high in and around the sink and I couldn't work out if there were more cats here or if the cats from the other room had followed us. Something fast and black darted across the floor and out of sight in a second. I was tired and hot and wanted to escape but there was no clear route to a door. The sweet rotten smell hung heavily in the air and my stomach lurched. I pushed through past the mess and clutter, flung the back door open just in time and was sick.

We hunched down at the bottom of the back garden. It was still hot, but a relief to be outside. Jon asked if I wanted that drink but I said no thanks, I was all right now. My mouth was dry and I could taste sick when I swallowed but I wouldn't be able to drink from anything in that house. I had a lot of questions to ask but I knew to take my time. If it wasn't general knowledge learnt from a book you couldn't rush Jon.

I slowly asked my questions, and slowly got some answers. They had been offered help many times and his grandparents had been threatened with care homes for years. He had been threatened with being taken into care himself a few times. They had dealt with it by not opening the door or reading any post. 'Like my dad,' I told him. That was why it had taken so long for Jon to answer the door: he wasn't supposed to. Jon did his bit, always turning up at school and keeping out of trouble, keeping his head down and doing his work. I asked what they did for money and Jon said they had some from when his grandparents sold their land when they retired from farming. He was given a few pounds each week for food and made it stretch. He looked worried. He said he thought it was starting to get low. He tore up a clump of grass and and let it fall back to the ground.

'We get on, you know, it's not always been like this.'

He pointed at the house. 'I mean, they've not always been so old and ill. They took me in when my mum died and for years they've looked after me. It's just been these last couple of years that they've got so bad.'

'Don't you want any help though?' I asked. 'Me and Dad could make things easier I'm sure we could.'

Jon shook his head quickly. 'They've changed these last couple of years. They've got scared somehow. They don't like outsiders, they don't like the council, they don't like anybody coming round. You can't come back and you can't bring your dad here.'

He was agitated, blinking fast and one hand scratching the top of other. The skin was red and breaking. I reached across and pulled his hands apart. I was sorry I had come. I didn't want to make it worse. I told him not to worry, I wouldn't come back. 'Why have you stopped coming to see us though?' He looked to the track that approached the house.

'They've been back again.'

You can only run so fast down a steep hill

My mum was manic depressive. She went through different phases and levels of illness but there was a basic pattern. She would start becoming manic, this would escalate until it reached a peak and then she'd hit a wall and drop into depression. Slowly she would come out of this. Things would be normal, sometimes for months, and then, eventually, it would all start again.

When mum thought I was old enough to understand

what she went through, she sat me down one night and described what happened to her. She called them her 'episodes'.

She started talking about when she 'speeded up'. She called it her manic side, her mania. As she was telling me, she became excited, her eyes sparkled and she had to stop herself from grinning. She pulled herself to the edge of her chair and leant forward with her arms on her knees.

'It's like knowing everything in the world at once. It feels like I am in complete control and have the power to do anything. My thoughts are faster and all my senses are more intense. It seems like every blade of grass is in exactly the right place, every bird is in the perfect tree. Every person I meet seems so full of promise. It feels like I can do anything. If I wanted to write a book, I could do it. If I wanted to climb a mountain, it would be easy.'

In one manic episode she read a book that moved her so much, seemed so important and vital to her, that the next morning she went to the bookshop and waited for it to open. She was disappointed when the shop only had a couple of copies in stock, but she ordered twenty more. They were going to be sent to friends and family, posted out to people so they could see the importance of this book. By the time the bookshop phoned to say her order had arrived she had crashed. She was in bed, unable to get up, so Dad went to collect the books. They sat in our spare room, evidence of her mania. A few were given away, but in her calmness she seemed embarrassed by the idea.

The mania would manifest itself in other ways. She decided to write her own book. For a few days this was all she did. She was locked away, typing, typing, typing. My dad had to take her drinks, take her food and ask her to come to bed and rest. She didn't listen to him though. I would go to the toilet in the early hours and see light slipping out from under the spare-room door. I could hear her fingers still racing over the keys. She had piles of reference books surrounding her and a mass of paper to her left showing how much she had written in such a short period of time. I asked her the next day what the book was about. She stopped typing for a few seconds and considered before replying. 'It's hard to pin it down. It's about lots of things. Little things and big things. How everything interconnects, how everything works.' I left her, pulsing away at the keyboard. She never did finish it. The crash came too soon.

I often asked if I could read it but I was never allowed. 'When it's finished, love' was always the reply, but I didn't see her write any more. She didn't seem interested in what she had started. I found it and read some of it anyway. It was confusing. There were parts I recognised and understood from our life but there were parts that made no sense to me. It seemed full of tangents and dead ends. I thought at the time I was just too young to understand.

She continued with her description but became quieter. 'After a while though, it starts to feel like you are moving and thinking too fast, you are no longer in control but are being controlled. It goes from being in charge of every thought in your head, every sinew in your body, to having no control at all. Thoughts aren't being formed in your head, they're being flung into your head. It's hard to keep up with everything.'

She was wary as she described this side of the illness. She talked about it like it was a misbehaving child – like it needed to be watched all the time. She described how she drove home late one night from a friend's house.

'All the houses I passed were dark and all I could see were sad people sat in black rooms, swallowed by unhappiness. Outside each room, guarding or keeping prisoner, was a large black dog. I couldn't shake the image. Even in daylight the next day that's all I could see.'

She told me it hurt to be depressed, that it's not like feeling down or sad or unhappy, that it's all of those combined and multiplied by thousands. She said, 'At the bottom of a bad period of depression, deep down into it, you see no way out. You are as far away from a way out as you have ever been and you can only see yourself going further down. It's very, very nearly unbearable. Sometimes for some people it becomes absolutely unbearable.'

She realised what she had said and came to hug me and smiled and said, 'Don't worry about me, love. Don't worry about me like that, ever. That's just not in me that isn't. And I'm doing well; I've been so much better since the last time, haven't I?'

We only want to help

When Jon said 'they' he meant Duerdale Social Services. There were two of them, he said. A middle-aged man and a younger woman. He said they banged on the door and tried to peer through the gaps in between the newspaper-covered windows. He said they smiled all the time and shouted through the letterbox, 'Mr Mansfield? Mrs Mansfield? Jon! Is anyone there? We need to come in and see you.' Jon hadn't seen them before, they were new, and he didn't like the look of them. They seemed keen he said. His granddad told him to get upstairs, to stay out of sight of the townies. So he hid in a dirty room full of tat and dust until he finally heard the car drive off down the fell track and back towards town.

He wasn't happy though. He told me he knew they would come back. Over the years he had come into contact with lots of social workers and he knew the ones who just filled in the forms and went back home to watch TV, have a drink and fall asleep on the couch and think no more of it until they were required to try again. He knew the ones who would write 'Visit attempted' and then two weeks later make the same half-hearted effort. But these two weren't like that. They had gone round the back and tried the door. They had shielded their eyes from the sun and looked up at the bedroom windows. They went back to the car and checked notes and looked back to the house and consulted and wondered. They shook their heads and slowly climbed back into their car. They had lingered, he said. They meant business.

We sat in a silence for a few minutes and I tried to blink away the question that kept buzzing into my head. It seemed cruel, but then I thought about the smell. And the filthy rooms and the cats and the two old people, dirty and dying by degrees in their chairs and in the end I just blurted it out. I asked if it would be such a bad thing. I asked if things could be any worse. Jon held my gaze. He spoke like he was talking to a child. Slowly and clearly he told me that of course things could be worse.

Gaskin, hock

My dad had started a project. I found drawings and plans in his workroom when I went in to steal some paint. They were laid out on his fourth work surface: The Creative Space. Scattered in front of me were sketches of horses. Drawings of the legs, of the head and the body. They were done from different angles, all with measurements and notes. The pictures were broken down into sections and labelled: 'crest, barrel, flank, gaskin, hock'. He always started with sketches. He would tell me that 'art is in the detail', as he slaved over the third draft of a design.

Laid next to the plans was a map of Duerdale Valley and he'd put a cross through the north-west corner of Brungerley Forest. The trees start only a couple of miles out of town and run for miles. Jon told me that it was quite famous locally. It was said that in the Middle Ages an old spinster lived there. Of course, an old woman living alone in the forest could only mean one thing: a witch. The locals agreed she should be put on trial but the trial never happened. When the magistrates turned up to take her to court they found her hanging from one of the trees on the edge of her camp. It was never discovered whether she killed herself or whether one of the locals got to her first. Ever since then there had been stories of witches from other areas visiting the forest as a pilgrimage, to pay their respects. There were rumours of a yearly gathering and some people believed it still went on to this day. Jon said we should visit the forest one day, that some of the trees were massive.

I smiled down at the diagrams and sketches. This was a good sign, a good thing. I waited until teatime the next day. I was sat with my pie and chips and Dad had his whisky. I blew on a hot crust of pie and said, 'I saw your drawings.'

He looked up, surprised.

'Of the horses?'

I nodded.

'Oh . . . right'

'They look good.'

'Thanks.'

He lifted the whisky up to his mouth but pulled the glass away without drinking.

'It's an idea I had years ago but never did anything with. Do you remember the rocking horses I made?'

I nodded.

'Well, I got the idea making those. They were always my favourite toys to carve. Something to get stuck into. But of course you have to stick it on some rockers and make sure it's safe. It's a toy, not a work of art.'

He looked at me to see if I was still with him.

'I wanted to make a carving without any restrictions. A big bloody wooden horse. They can be huge, you know, and if you saw one of them charging at you, well, you wouldn't be hanging around. Saucepan eyes, teeth the size of piano keys and legs that could kick your head off your shoulders.'

He took a short swig. 'When it's finished I want it to stand outside, not sat in a gallery or exhibition hall getting dusty.'

He leant forward, excited now.

'Not in the middle of a park though, or on top of a hill. Just somewhere someone would occasionally stumble across. Almost like a secret. That's why I've chosen Brungerley Forest. There are miles of unmarked tracks and dead ends, tracks that peter out, tracks that you aren't even sure are tracks or just gaps between the trees. You can walk for days and not end up in the same place or walk for twenty minutes in one direction and end up back where you started. It's disorientating.'

I'd noticed he'd been going out more but he hadn't said where and I hadn't asked. I was just pleased because going out more meant drinking less.

'There would be no signs, no explanations, no interviews in the local paper. It would just appear. I often spoke about this with your mum. We both loved the idea but I never got further than just talking about it.'

I was stung by the mention of her. We hadn't talked about her since she died but it was the most he'd spoken about anything in months and I wanted to keep him going.

'What kind of wood will you use?' I asked.

'English oak; it will need to be well treated but it's one of the best for outdoor carving. It will last for years.'

'Will you need permission from the council?'

'Probably, if they knew about it. But who's going to tell them?'

We both smiled at the outlaw still lurking in him.

'How will it stay standing in the wind?'

'I'll have to root the feet into the ground. It can be done. I'll fix the hooves to iron rods and dig those deep into the ground.'

'When will you start?'

'I already have.'

'Can me and Jon help?'

'Course you can, I'll need help.'

We grinned at each other and I saw deep in his eyes for the first time in months the glimmer of a twinkle.

An awful thing to think

Sometimes I'm too angry to sleep and sometimes I'm avoiding the dreams. And sometimes, for whatever reason, sleep just won't come. It feels like my brain is wired to a slide show, flicking and jumping from one image to the next. When I have a night like this I just accept I won't be sleeping. These are always thinking times and sometimes thoughts wander and scurry where you wouldn't normally let them or want them to go.

This particular night my brain kept being drawn to this question: if I could have chosen who came to pick me up from art club that day, who would I have had driving the car, Mum or Dad? It was a horrible thing to think about but I couldn't shake the question away. It kept jumping back into my head and it seemed like the only thing to do was address it so at least then it might leave me alone and let me rest.

I started slowly and I started with the positives. Mum was more outgoing, more affectionate and communicative. She was fun and silly but she always looked after me and could tell when I was upset or worried about something. My dad is calmer, more balanced and kind. He is gentle and creative and could be fun too. Of course they both had their other sides to consider. Mum had her manic depression to contend with, which meant that one day she could be climbing the walls with energy and the next day shrunken and shattered and in bed, curtains drawn, and Dad and me tiptoeing around the house, talking in whispers. Dad has always been quieter. He would never ignore me but he was often there in body with his mind elsewhere, lost in thoughts that seemed to entrance him and carry him off over the hills. There was also the drinking to consider, but I didn't think it was fair to include this. His proper drinking started afterwards, and who knows how Mum would have reacted if it had been me and her left alone in a crumbling house in a crap town.

And I think that's the point really. I'm not sure you can ever get a true answer. The dad I have now isn't the dad I had before. He's a different person and it would have been the same for Mum if it'd been Dad that had disappeared in a second. She would have changed somehow. Like we have changed. One person is gone and the ones left behind are altered so everything and everybody is different. And what I never really understood before any of this happened is that death means disappearance. A sudden full stop and a big empty nothing. It's the ultimate vanishing trick.

Work and industry

It was a couple of days after my visit and Jon took me to a part of Duerdale I'd never been before. We walked from the town centre, behind the Town Hall and across Duerdale Recreational Park (which is a fenced-off area of gravel with three swings, a slide, and a scruffy patch of grass with a sign that says 'No Ball Games'). When we pushed through the gate on the far side of the park my surroundings were immediately unfamiliar but Jon knew exactly where he was heading. He walked fast and I scuttled along trying to keep up whilst drinking in as many of the new sights as I could. On the lookout for ideas for new paintings. After a few rows of terraced houses we reached old red mills that were tall and stretched on for ever. We cut through between two giant mills on a tiny cobbled passage and I stopped and held my arms out. I could touch both walls with flat palms but I couldn't decide if it felt like I was pushing the mills apart or stopping them close in together. I looked up at the thin line of sky that slotted between the walls and every bone in my body felt tiny and fragile. I hurried on, catching back up with Jon, keen now to be in open space. We left the cobbled passage at the next ginnel and rejoined the main road.

The mills were enormous. One building alone had a sign that showed it housed a plastic-mouldings firm, a carpet factory and a graphic printers. We passed along on the road, through the noise of booming radio voices and the clunk-clattering of machines. Work noises jumped out from different windows and echoed and spun in the road, bouncing back off high brick walls causing a cacophony in the street. We crossed a dirty river that ran alongside the mills. Its banks were littered with junk: mattresses, prams, cookers and other debris, rusted and wasted out of recognition years before. The buildings grew into a state of disrepair the further we walked away from town and the screeching noise of the businesses gradually faded away behind us, dwindling to a murmured nothing. The final mill we passed looked like it had been abandoned the day it shipped its last loom of cotton; the entrance was boarded up and the windows were smashed. Only one window had survived intact and Jon pointed it out, a small corner window on the second floor. We both stared up at it for a while, wondering how it had escaped, it was an easy enough target, and then Jon started walking on again and I fell into step alongside him. I had an idea where we were headed but I hadn't asked. Jon was still annoyed with me, I could tell, and I had a feeling I was about to be taught a lesson and that it was my duty to suffer in silence. We passed the last deserted mill and walked out into open wasteland. More junk congregated here, some of it in piles, some randomly scattered. We zig-zagged our way through it all, crossed the busy circular road and arrived at the estates. The houses were small and squat, all regulation size and made out of grey breezeblock brick, the kind of brick that darkens in the rain. There was a low grey sky hovering above it all and for a few moments I was almost grateful for my disintegrating house. As we passed the regularly spaced road ends we could see kids further down in the maze of streets, wheelying on bikes, sitting on walls, looking for anything to do. Jon kept his head down and walked faster and I was right with him. We only slowed when we had passed the last clutch of houses and left the estates behind.

It was just starting to get dark now and our surroundings took on a dusty, moonlike glow. We were at the opposite end of town now, as far away from my house as I'd been, and almost back in open countryside. The road turned from tarmac to gravel and we crunched our way on. Eventually, through the fading light, I saw a large dark building ahead. And I knew that was our destination. Jon was walking straight towards it, head down, in silence.

Brick windows

The house stood square and defiant. Front door in the middle, three rows of windows on either side. Big and ugly. It was large and detached, surrounded by trees and shrubs and with fields all around. 'Georgian,' Jon said as we trudged closer. The nearer we got the less impressive the house revealed itself to be. Paint was peeling and moss and weeds grew out of the brickwork. It had a functional, institutional look, like it was kept standing on the minimal possible budget. I noticed that some of the windows were bricked up and pointed them out to Jon and he said that would have been done years ago. He said that there was a window tax, introduced by William III and the more windows you had the more tax you paid, so people just blocked them up. There were bars on the windows of the ground floor and security cameras over the front door. I wondered if they were to stop people breaking in or escaping or both.

We stopped at a low fence, where the track continued through a gateway to the house and Jon said we'd better not go any further. He pointed to a large sign that stood just behind the fence. I had to squint to read it in the grey gloom: 'St Liam's Crisis and Respite Unit'. The local children's home. He was showing me how things could be worse. I took a deep breath and tried not to be too down on the place; it could be brilliant for all I knew. I shrugged, 'It might be all right.' Jon pulled two newspaper cuttings out of his pocket, probably taken from his grandparents' collection, and handed them to me. One was old, yellow and brittle and the other one was more recent, jet-black ink not yet faded. The older article had the headline: 'Local Care Home: Den of Abuse'. It was from five years ago and according to the article the people involved had been jailed after a full investigation and the care home was under new management. Still, I looked up at the building and a goose walked across my grave. I shivered it off. The more recent piece was from the point of view of local residents from the estates we had just passed.

The *Duerdale Advertiser* said the home had started a new scheme and as well as local children St Liam's took in 'troubled and violent adolescents, recently released from secure accommodation'. There were complaints of gangs congregating, vandalism and residents feeling threatened. Running battles between the estate kids and the kids from St Liam's were reported. One resident, who wanted to remain anonymous, was quoted as saying, 'We daren't come out at night. There are marauding gangs, smashing cars and windows and fighting each other. They're all on drink and drugs. We didn't have any trouble before they shipped this lot here. The council should close it down and send them somewhere else; this is the wrong place for them. We don't have the resources to deal with them here.' The article said that one youth had been taken back to a young offenders' institution after he'd stabbed another resident in a fight. I handed the cuttings back to Jon.

'This is where they'd put me,' he said. We looked at each other and then back to the building. Neither of us spoke. After a few seconds Jon turned around and started walking back towards a quickly darkening Duerdale. I hurried to follow, not wanting to be left behind.

All carved up

The carving was taking shape. It was huge. And muscular. The body was massive; my head only came to the top of the legs. I expected the muscles to ripple and sweat at any moment. Me and Jon didn't really help much at all; it was clearly my dad's project and he didn't need any help and we let him get on with it. He worked regularly and with intent and didn't really need us.

I could see it was working; it was obvious. It's the same with a painting. Sometimes it comes together and other times it just doesn't happen, no matter how hard you try. You can plan the painting, decide on the colours, shapes and style and see the finished work in your head. But you don't get close. Something doesn't spark. The moon was in the wrong orbit or the stars weren't aligned. Other times, it's as easy as opening a door. I could tell, looking at Dad's carving, at the flared nostrils, the big oval eyes and the kicking legs, that it would be the best thing he'd ever done. He had to work in the evenings; the days were taken up with making the usual toys and the weekends were used to sell them at markets around the county. He was working hard and that was good. He was focused. It didn't stop the drinking though. The bottle was never too far away, but at least now he was doing something whilst he drank.

The carving dominated the workroom. It stood in the middle with all the other work pushed to the sides. When you walked into the room the horse reared over you, with a fierce expression and high kicking legs. Jon seemed almost afraid of it; he would hurry past, duck around it, like he was afraid his presence might jolt it into life. He was also mesmerised by it. Once he was in the room and at a safe distance, he would stare intently, walk a few steps to the left or right and stare again.

I could see small changes in my dad when he was

working. Not in his appearance or anything he said, but in the way he moved. For months he'd been dragging his body around reluctantly with him, like it was a weight to carry, even though he looked only half his own size. But when he was working on the carving he was different. He was still as silent but he moved with an energy that hadn't been there for a long time. He was absorbed and purposeful and I could see that he wasn't brooding, that he was concentrating and planning and creating. It made me relax, made me a little less fearful. It was good to see.

Clumsy creatures at dawn

The three of us visited the site he had chosen for the carving to stand. We went early on a Sunday morning, just as dawn was breaking, and grabbed Jon from the end of his lane on the way. Dad wanted to see what the site would look like first thing and he needed to get off to a local market to try and sell some toys later. The valley was still lying in thick mist when we set off but we were above it all on top of the fell, looking down onto the white valley. Only the two cement chimneys, a church spire and the tops of the tallest trees popped out through the top and Duerdale looked like an ancient town given up to the sea.

I knew there was a car park at the town side of the forest and I thought we were headed there. It was signposted from the town centre and had public toilets and a big board mapped with different walks. It seemed the obvious place to start but Dad drove straight past and kept going. We drove for a few miles and I was struck by how vast the forest was. The road got narrower and the trees loomed over us. We rose and fell on sharp, steep, little climbs and as the road carried us on my sleepy mind wandered and I began thinking about who had built these roads and when. All those men must be dead now, surely? Had they all lived locally or did teams of road builders travel around the country, laying their route out in front of them and never stopping? Who decided where you built the roads and who paid their wages? These half-thoughts skimmed the surface of my brain as the car carried us on, ducking and twisting beneath the trees. We didn't see another car or any walkers or anyone. We were alone, the only people awake and travelling through this ancient place. I wondered about the ages of the trees and realised that they would, more than likely, still be stood in the same place, under the same patch of sky long after me, Dad and Jon were dead.

Eventually Dad pulled over. We were at the back of the forest and miles away from town and miles away from the public entrance to the forest. We all climbed out and shook life back into our car-tired legs. We were stood in front of a rusty green gate. There was no wall or fence on either side, just two crumbling concrete gateposts holding it in place. It looked ridiculous, sat by itself on the edge of a forest in the middle of nowhere. Dad said it looked like an album cover from years ago. He asked if we were ready and we both nodded and followed him through the falling-down gateposts and into the forest.

The trees swallowed the light and we stood still, adjusting to the darkness. There was an absolute silence, a heavy calm and a feeling that if you had to speak you should speak in a whisper. The floor was carpeted with brown pine needles and green moss and was springy under foot and the air smelt of dry tree and cold mornings. After a few seconds considering, Dad moved slowly forward, squinting at his sketched map and looking up to check he was moving in the right direction. There didn't appear to be any track he was following as he weaved through the trees and it was uneven ground and the tree roots snaked across the forest floor and me and Jon kept our eyes on the ground. It was tough going. It felt like the roots were trying to grab us and pull us to the floor. Dad was more used to it and he had to stop and wait for us to catch up every few minutes.

Eventually I got surer on my feet and looked up to see what was overhead. It was a trick I learned from my mum. She said that every now and again, walking your usual route through town or to school, you should look up as you travelled instead of straight ahead, that you would see things you hadn't seen before. And she was right. The first time I walked through our old town and lifted my head up I saw things I'd never noticed in a town I'd lived in all my life. In the forest the trees stretched high and higher into the sky, disappearing out of sight and there was only the odd glimpse of sky poking through the canopy. It felt like we were indoors; it reminded me of the church on the day of my mum's funeral: ancient and powerful.

It took Jon a bit longer to get steady on his feet but eventually he settled into some kind of rhythm and started telling us about trees and their history. How, from the story of Adam and Eve up to today, trees were held in special regard because they start underneath the ground, push up into this world and appear to be stretching up towards heaven. He said that for some groups of people they were a symbol of the next life in this world. I told him I didn't believe in heaven and hell and the next life and we fell silent again and carried on, pushing through the trees.

We stirred the forest into life. There were birds singing a warning to each other: look out for the three clumsy creatures, sliding and crashing across the forest floor. I was sure I heard sounds of bigger animals amongst the trees but whenever I looked in the direction of the rustle there was nothing there, just a feeling that the second before I turned my head there had been.

I was worried about Jon. His coughing had got worse over the last few weeks and I could see he was starting to struggle. There were beads of sweat popping on his forehead but when I gave him my hand to help him up a steep climb his grip was cold and clammy. I didn't draw Dad's attention to it. He'd been a bit unsure about letting us come and I had to nag him. Thankfully he stopped for a break and leant against a tree and passed a bottle of water around. Jon sat down, grateful for the rest. I took a gulp of the water and asked, 'How are you going to get the carving all the way out here?' Dad laughed. 'Determination.' I passed the bottle to Jon who took a big swig. Dad told us, 'Not much further now and I have my own story about trees anyway.' He took a glance at his map, folded it back up and pushed forward.

Bannister

'When I was at school there was a cross-country race every year. It was for the oldest lads, those about to finish school, and it was always held at the end of the final term, just before the summer holidays. It was hard, about six miles long and tough terrain, up to the top of Lendep Hill and back down through Drumsford Wood. A killer. I doubt they could get away with it these days but it was a school tradition, seen as a final test before leaving the school, a graduation I suppose.'

He turned to see if we were listening, and I nodded at him to carry on, and we tried to keep up with his long strides.

'Mr Franks the PE teacher used to stay at the back, to make sure that everyone did the whole route so there wouldn't be anyone hiding near the school and then running back when they thought they'd waited long enough. There was another teacher at the top of the hill, marking everyone off as they passed and checking that everyone was still alive. As you can imagine some lads loved it and some hated it. I was looking forward to it; I found running easy and it would be good to get out of the classroom and away from all the teachers and the crowded corridors.

'When it was my turn it was a hot summer, broke records apparently. It was a roasting Thursday in the middle of July and we were told to take it steady, but there was no way they were going to cancel it. This year, at the top of the hill, as well as having someone checking us off, they had another teacher handing out water to stop us getting dehydrated.

'We set off to a cheer from the rest of the school and we all ran too fast across the playing fields before settling down to a sensible pace. The slow ones must have been halfway up Lendep Hill and the fast ones already descending when Doug Bannister finally turned up. He'd been at an interview for a job at a local business for when he finished with school, but he knew he would still have to do the run. Of course there was no one behind him. Mr Franks had set off with the rest of the year and he was barking at the slow ones to get a move on and pick their feet up and put some bloody effort in. Bannister was on the football and swimming teams so he was quite fit and apparently he set off at a good pace.

'I was doing well. I wasn't winning. A lad called Chris Lockton won every race; he was a member of a local club and trained three times a week. I was in second place though and feeling pretty good. There was a nice breeze at the top of the hill and I could see the school in the distance, some of the younger kids still on the school fields watching us run to our freedom. The second half was tougher than I expected with the steep descent and then through the winding woods but I stayed in second place and got some cheers when I finished.

'More and more people started finishing and we all

sat together on the field, feeling tired but happy. Some of the younger kids brought out buckets of cold water and we got them to throw them over us to cool us down. We'd heard that Bannister had set off after everyone else and we thought about him still climbing the steep slope of Lendep Hill in the hot sun as we lay on the grass, dripping in cold water and recovering. Eventually we heard Mr Franks's fog-horn voice shouting at the last few lads to sprint to the finish, where he finally got his glory and went flying past them all to boos and cheers from all of us.

'There wouldn't be any more lessons that day; it was considered enough that we had finished the run. We were all laughing and chatting, nearly finished with school and feeling grown up, just waiting for Bannister to finish. It got to a time when we expected him back but there was no sign. We waited another fifteen minutes and somebody said he was probably taking it easy; there was no point in him killing himself. And then Mrs Crawford and Mr Hunter turned up. They'd been at the top of the hill, handing out the water and marking people off as they passed. They asked what we were all doing still at the finish line, so we told them, mucking about, waiting for Bannister. They looked at each other and Mrs Crawford said that Doug had passed them ages ago, taken his water and seemed fine. They'd slowly walked back to the school after collecting all the empty plastic cups in bin bags. Even Mr Franks looked concerned and he was never bothered about anyone. He said that if Bannister had fallen it was most likely in the wood or on the descent so Chris and me should go back and check Drumsford Wood, he would miss out the wood and head straight to the bottom of Lendep Hill.

'The sun was at its hottest now, sending down hard heat. We took two flasks of water, one for us and one for Bannister, and set off fast across the school playing fields again. Mr Franks shouted at us to slow down, that he didn't want any more casualties. He was running twice as fast us in the other direction, straight to the foot of Lendep.'

Dad paused and turned to check we were still keeping up. He'd slowed down now he was telling a story and Jon had taken the chance to recover a little. He saw we were right with him, took a deep breath and continued.

'It was an adventure and we were excited. We didn't think anything really bad had happened to Doug, just a sprained ankle or cramp or something. I could tell Chris wanted to find him too. I think we both hoped he was in the wood and we would rescue him and take him back to school as heroes. A Hollywood graduation. We slowed down when we reached the wood; it was hard to keep the same pace on the rough tracks and it was nice to be in the shade. We took more care to look left and right; he may have tripped and fallen to one side of the path and the undergrowth was thick on both sides. I knew Chris was right behind me; I occasionally felt his hand on my shoulder as I had to slow and turn a sudden left or right. The tight track eventually opened up and began to arch left, a long gradual sweep, and we sped up again. I had just begun to lengthen my stride and looked up, plotting our course, when I saw him. Face down on the floor, arms spread out ahead of him, like he'd fallen whilst halting traffic. He was so still that I think I knew he was dead straight away. I stopped running in a step and Chris crashed into the back of me. He was about to complain when he looked up and saw Doug. We both stood still and stared. Doug's left leg splayed out to the side and it looked painful. I was sure he would have moved it if he could. We slowly walked up to him and I knelt down next to him and touched his shoulder and said, 'Doug . . . can you hear me?' There was no movement, no response. I touched his cheek and it was already turning a little cold. I didn't want to but I knew I had to so I turned his head towards us, and it was then I knew he was dead. His eyes stared right over my shoulder, not focusing, not moving. I heard Chris, a few steps behind me. He made a strange noise, a mixture of a groan and a yelp . . .'

Dad stopped walking and me and Jon came to a halt behind him. We stood waiting, watching his back . . . Eventually Jon spoke. He asked the question I wanted to ask: 'How did he die?'

Dad turned and looked from Jon to me and back to Jon again.

'He had tripped on a tree root and fallen onto the stump of a young birch tree. The stump punctured his heart and killed him. We didn't know that at the time though. We just knew there was a lot of blood and he was dead. Chris said he would go and get help. He told me to wait with Doug. I remember thinking two things simultaneously: why do I have to wait here and how are they going to help? But then I saw the look on Chris's face. He was terrified, and already backing away. I could see his legs were wet and he followed my eyes down and saw what'd happened. He looked ashamed. I told him not to be daft. He took his T-shirt off, rubbed his legs dry, threw it away and ran off, nearly falling over as he set off. I didn't know what to do. I sat down away from Doug with my back against a tree but that seemed disrespectful somehow, so I moved closer and sat cross-legged next to him but that felt strange, I was too close so . . . I stood up . . . and waited for them to come.'

The clearing

We walked on in silence for a few minutes. My dad noticed the quiet, he cleared his throat and laughed. 'So think on, no running in heavily wooded areas, watch your step.' We nodded and kept our eyes fixed on the forest floor, stepping carefully over roots and searching out any tree stumps. Five minutes later he came to a stop and nodded ahead. We could see a clearing through the trees, straight ahead. The forest had been tightly packed all the time we'd been walking. If one of us had run off in any direction we would have disappeared from sight within a few seconds. This was the first bit of open space we had come across. It was a find. We walked forward, out of the gloom and into the bright light of the open space. It was almost perfectly round, like someone had drawn around a giant glass rim and cut out all the trees. The mist had cleared and we were suddenly underneath a big, bright September sky. Jon walked to the middle of the clearing, looked around at the surrounding trees and leant back till he almost fell over. He looked up at the sky and said, 'Perfect.'

'It is,' my dad agreed, 'but logistically . . . a bloody nightmare.'

He sat down with his back to a tree and passed the water around again. He explained how he thought it would work. He would make the carving in pieces, assemble it together at the house and make sure everything fitted. He would then take it apart and bring the pieces here one by one. He would keep them under tarpaulin and, when they were all delivered, put them back together in the clearing. 'I reckon I've got a few weeks of good weather left.' He looked up at the sky. 'An Indian summer they say.'

I asked if people would ever find it here and he told me that didn't really matter. 'We'll know it's here and every now and again someone will stumble across it. I'm not sure they'll ever be able to find it again though. I had to makes notes after I found this place and even then, at one point I thought I'd never see it again. I struggled the first couple of times I came back. But that's the beauty. They may even begin to doubt it was ever here. You know, a couple of people see it, tell their friends, they never find it, it could become an urban myth . . . in a forest . . .' He laughed and asked if we were ready to head home. He consulted his notes for a few seconds and then we stepped back into the dark forest and stumbled and slipped our way back to the car. We drove back through Duerdale and a lazy Sunday morning with people walking dogs and picking up newspapers. We dropped Jon off at the end of his track and were back at the house by mid-morning. Just the time I would normally be getting up on a Sunday. Shattered, I crawled into bed and quickly fell asleep.

New trainers

It was the next Saturday afternoon and I was sat in the kitchen with Jon. We were talking about Doug Bannister and what a horrible way it was to die, puncturing your heart on a tree stump alone in a wood. We wondered if he would have died instantly or if he slowly bled to death shouting out for help. I wondered if there was a moment when he realised that was it: he really was dying and he'd lived all the life he was going to live. I tried to imagine how that would feel but it's impossible. How can you know how you will feel seconds before you die? You hear that a peace descends and there is a light at the end of a tunnel and heavenly music playing and crap like that. I think that's a trick. A lie spread to keep people calm. Like when the doctor says it won't hurt, so you relax, and then he jams the massive needle into your arm and you aren't struggling because the pain takes you by surprise. I think watching death coming to get you must be the most terrifying thing in the world. You are about to come to a stop and every-thing else around you is going to carry on. And let's be honest, all these people who talk about the beautiful experience and the twinkling lights, well they don't actually die in the end do they, so why would anyone listen to them? Give me a dead man's account and then I'll start to take notice. I thought of my mum, one second singing along to the radio and the next gone. If it did happen like that, in a split second, like they said at the inquest, then that was a good thing. No terror, no pain, just driving along and then nothing. Blam. It should just have been a split second sixty years later that's all.

We'd been sat quietly for a few minutes when Jon broke the silence. He pointed at the open shoebox sat in the middle of the table and said, 'New trainers.' My dad had bought me them in town that morning and they were in their box, on the kitchen table. They were a bright white with green soles and green trims. They looked good. I wasn't sure if he could really afford them but he'd got the idea into his head that he wanted to buy me something and he'd almost dragged me into town and made me choose. 'Anything you want, what do you need? Music? Paint? Clothes?' I didn't need anything but he seemed excited to be treating me and we were stood outside the sports shop so trainers seemed the obvious solution. I tried to find a cheap pair but he kept steering me towards the new ranges. He asked which I would choose if money were no object, if we'd won the lottery. So I thought sod it and was honest and pointed to the white and green trainers sat in the middle of the display in the window. They were too expensive but he made me try them on anyway, squeezed my big toes to check they fitted, and told the shop assistant we would take them.

Jon reached across and took one of the shoes from the box and passed it from hand to hand. 'Light, aren't they?' he said. He brought it up to his nose and inhaled. 'Smells good.' He tucked it back in the box carefully. I told him to try them on. He shook his head. He didn't want to, he said; they were brand new. I shrugged and told him that I wasn't bothered. After a bit more persuading he pulled off his old, battered, brown shoes and slipped his feet into the trainers, carefully threaded the laces and tied them up. He tied each foot firmly, straightened the tongues and looked up at me, unsure what to do next. I told him to give them a run around. He stood up and walked a few stiff steps towards the kitchen door. He stopped, turned around, looked at me and said, 'It's like wearing moon boots!' He walked around the kitchen table a couple of times, getting used to the feel of the trainers on his feet. They were two sizes too big for him but it didn't matter. He broke into big, bounding strides, like he was jumping from dry land to dry land. Then he hopped on his left foot in a clockwise direction around the table, and swapped to his right and came back the other way. He looked at me with a wide grin and said, 'These are brilliant!'

At that moment the neurons fizzed and popped in my brain and I couldn't believe I hadn't thought of it before. I told Jon to follow me upstairs. I rummaged through my wardrobe, chucking jeans, T-shirts, shirts and jumpers onto the bed. I even found a pair of trainers and put them on the pile. Everything was in pretty good condition; I'd had a growth spurt shortly after me and Mum had bought most of this stuff and none of it had been worn much at all. Jon sat on the bed, mainly ignoring me, his focus still on the green and white trainers on his feet. When I found everything I thought was too small for me but not too big for Jon I pushed the pile over to him and told him he could have them, that they were no good to me any more. He looked at me like I was insane and shook his head and said no, he couldn't have them. I told him that it wasn't a big deal, that it was just old clothes. It took a while to convince him that I was sure, and no, my dad *really* wouldn't mind, that he wouldn't even notice. And then Jon began to relax. He spent the rest of the afternoon trying the clothes on in different combinations and grinning at himself in the mirror.

Lithium

My mum finally got properly diagnosed after the apples-and-oranges incident. She was told she suffered from bipolar disorder and was prescribed lithium to help control her manic episodes. She said the lithium helped; it kept her stable and stopped her getting ahead of herself. Dad had taken her to the doctor a few times before, but she always went reluctantly and we later found out she never told the doctor the full extent of her symptoms. She was only ever diagnosed with stress and panic attacks and given a booklet on relaxation techniques and some beta-blockers.

Everything changed when Dad got a phone call from the police saying that they had Mum down at the station. She hadn't been arrested but it was important that he came in for a chat with them. He bundled me into the car and drove faster than I'd seen him drive. He flung the car to a stop right outside the police station and told me to wait where I was. He strode up the steps and banged through the doors. I sat in the cold car, watching my breath mist up the windows and wondered what was going on inside.

I found out later that the police had been called to the High Street where they'd found Mum handing out apples and oranges to passers-by. She'd bought cases of them from a local organic dealer and was stopping people as they passed and lecturing them on the nutrients and vitamins contained in fruit and how important it was to feed the body and brain with the right kind of food. She was preaching about how supermarkets fly in apples from America even though we have wonderful apples in our own orchards. 'Think about your carbon footprint,' she told them and took a big bite from a red apple. She was quite insistent, trying to push the fruit in people's pockets if they just walked past and it was obvious that something was wrong. One of the local shopkeepers had tried to calm her, made her a cup of tea and told her to come in and sit down. When she brushed him away and carried on as frantically as before he rang the police. The police told my dad that she had scared some people, that her manner had been intense. They said she needed to see a doctor. Dad knew that; he'd been trying to get her help for ages. This time, Mum agreed.

As usual, the next day she was the opposite of how she had been only a few hours before. She looked exhausted as Dad helped her into the car. She was dressed in a big jumper and jeans and looked as slow and frail as an old woman. Dad went in with her to see the doctor. The doctor asked Mum what the problem was and she told him everything. It took twenty minutes. The doctor nodded a lot and made little scribbles on his pad. When Mum had finished and sunk low into the chair Dr Hanson told her that she displayed all the symptoms of bipolar disorder. He said he would like to send her to a special clinic that deals with the illness but there was a waiting list of eighteen months. So he sent her back to us with a suitcase of drugs and strict instructions to rest. He made sure that Mum went back to see him every two weeks though, to monitor how she was feeling and to see if they needed to change the prescription.

Word had got out and travelled around the school and by the next day everyone was talking about the mental apples-and-oranges woman. Nobody mentioned it to me, but I heard conversations fall suddenly quiet as I walked past and I got a lot more looks than usual and my friend Ian got in a fight at lunch but wouldn't tell me why. Dad sat me down that night and told me he was sorry if Mum's behaviour had caused me any problems or embarrassment at school but it was just something we would have to deal with. I told him not to worry, that if anyone said anything I'd tell them to fuck off. He laughed and told me that I had the right idea.

Things did get gradually better but the lithium was no magic cure. It was no magic pill that solved all

Mum's problems. The dose was too high at first and she was almost sedated; she was like a zombie. She found it hard to keep track of conversation and her sentences would trail off before they were finished. The doctor reduced the prescription and in the end it did work. She was calmer and more balanced but sometimes she seemed sad. I asked her once what the lithium was like and she said it was a necessary evil. She said that it made her feel like she'd been driven to a spectacular view on top of a cliff but told she must stay in the car so she couldn't feel the wind and couldn't smell the sea. And it made her mouth taste metallic and she had been sick in public a couple of times, which was embarrassing, but it did stop her speeding up and spinning out of control.

She told me, 'I do miss the thrill though, the excitement and the feelings I had before. It really did feel like anything was possible and now everything just seems a little flat.' She gave me a hug and said, 'Still it's better than being the mental fruit lady, isn't it?'

A wonderful artist/Slack Jaw

The last few days of the holidays sped past faster than I thought possible and I tried to prepare myself for school. I realised, though, that it isn't something you can prepare for and I just spent the time nervous and irritable and not hungry. And when the first school day dawned the weather matched my mood. The town was cowering under black clouds that lagged so low they almost rested on rooftops. The wind swung into the surrounding hills and bounced back into town with more energy than before, like a fly in a war with a window. The gusts brought the cold hill rain back down from the fells and into the narrow streets and water shot at random angles, striking people in their faces and shooting up their sleeves.

Dad drove me down into town and stopped a sensible distance from the school despite the weather. We'd agreed that he would drive me to school in the mornings and I would get the bus back at the end of the day. That way he would be back at the house before nine o'clock and would be able to work right through until the evening. I was surprised to find that there was a bus that ran out past our house but Jon said that the council had to provide it for children who lived in rural areas. He said that it was called the sheepshaggers' express and that he'd always been the last person on the bus, but now that would be me.

Dad wished me luck and I climbed out of the car in my horribly new uniform and braced myself against the weather. I walked towards the school gates as kids shot past me as fast as the rain, shouting and squealing, running to get indoors, to get out of the weather, excited to be back at school. I did as the letter instructed and found my way to the school office and reported my presence. The lady behind the glass screen cocked her head and smiled and told me that I was the only new starter in my year and they were pleased to have me. She took my letter and told me to go and wait in reception and my form teacher would come and collect me. She told me that I had Mr Hartley and I shouldn't worry because he was lovely. I wanted to tell her that I didn't give a toss how lovely Mr Hartley was but she was too nice to upset so I tried to smile and look less like a thunderstorm. I pushed my way back to the reception through throngs of kids pouring through the corridors. I was aware of eyes on me. From head to toe. Assessing. Calculating. Considering. But I couldn't blame them. There's something obvious about a new kid that you can spot a mile off and you just have to look. Everything about them gives them away and there are so many clues. The shiny new uniform, itchy and unworn. The tie, knotted like kids did at your old school but not how it's done here. The walk, trying to convey confidence and calm and ending up nowhere near either. It probably would be easier to give all new kids a siren that you strap on your head for the first day and get it over with.

I was only waiting a couple of minutes before Mr Hartley swept into reception and dragged me off. He walked quickly down corridors and up and down stairs and spent the time telling me how refreshing it was to have a new pupil to work with, how he hoped I would enjoy my time at Duerdale High and make the most of all the opportunities presented to me. He swept around one last corner and we arrived: Room 19, turquoise blue door. He paused for dramatic effect, did a mock-horror face and then swung the door open and wheeled me to the front of the classroom. He shouted for quiet and when the noise eventually tapered into silence he rested his hands on my shoulders.

'This is our new pupil, a Mr Luke Redridge.'

Thirty-two faces stared at me.

'And I hear on the grapevine that he is, and I quote, a *wonderful* artist, so let's make him feel very welcome!'

My heart sank and right on cue one of the boys at the back of the class coughed out 'Ponce!' which raised a few laughs and I forced a smile to try and show that I didn't take myself too seriously. I was shown my seat and given my timetable and saw that I had to survive Science, English, French and Geography before I was released for the day. The bell rang and Mr Hartley told Leanne Cunliffe to make sure I knew where I was going and then strode out of the room. Leanne Cunliffe looked at me, picked up her bag and walked off. I followed, five steps behind, hoping that she was on her way to the Science lab too. For the rest of the morning the other teachers barely seemed to notice that they had a new pupil. They hunted out textbooks and exercise books, told me to find a seat and tried to hide the fact they were miserable to be back at work.

I was in the same year as Jon but not the same classes and I spent most of the first day on the lookout for him. We couldn't even meet at lunch because I got sent to the office to fill in a bunch of forms about next of kin, emergency contacts, school trips and allergies. It was strange to only write Dad's name on each sheet and when I handed the forms back they seemed only half finished and incomplete and I thought I might get told to do them again. I didn't see Jon at all until just before the last lesson. I was walking down the main school corridor, along with loads of other kids, and I could see, further ahead, the back of a familiar head bobbing along. I tried to catch up with him but it was hard work trying to push past the groups of kids flooding my way and I never did get to him. But I did see what happened. And it explained his silences. As he passed one group of older kids, a stray leg kicked out and got him on the shin. When he passed the next group he got an elbow in his side, and just before he disappeared around the corner and out of sight he got a quick slap to the back of his head. And it only took a few minutes into my next lesson to learn the name Jon was commonly known as. A big, greasy-skinned kid called Kieran Judd leant across my desk and asked me, 'Do you live on the fell with that weird kid, that spastic kid? Slack Jaw Jon?'

When the final bell rang I found our small bus idling outside and climbed on. I saw Jon, sitting quietly, third row down, his face set. I sat down next to him and we watched the other kids walking past *baaa*-ing at the bus. I didn't mention to him that I'd seen what'd happened in the corridor. And I didn't tell him what Kieran Judd had said. We both stared out of the window of the half-empty bus as the town disappeared and the few country bumpkins got delivered back home at the end of the day.

Wild, wooden and white

Dad called me and Jon to the workroom. It was the unveiling. It was a dark windy evening and he'd lit candles and placed them around the room. The flames flickered and fell over and worked their way upright again as draughts swung through the outhouse. Shadows jumped and slid across the white walls and it felt special. It was the perfect atmosphere. The carving stood in the centre of the room covered in large dust sheets, and I was nervous. We hadn't seen anything for a while. Dad, as usual, had become more secretive as he got close to finishing. He always was when he was working on a special piece of work. The carving had finally come together in the last couple of weeks and I hoped that it was as good as I wanted it to be. I was desperate not to be disappointed.

He asked if we were ready and we both nodded. Jon stood behind me a little, as if he was unsure of what exactly lurked beneath the sheet and wanted that extra yard for protection. Dad carefully pulled away the covers and let them fall to the floor and I swear I heard Jon's mouth drop open. The horse was stood on his hind legs with his front legs kicking high in the air. The hooves were higher than my head. His teeth were bared, his nostrils wide and his eyes wild. He was painted a dusty white, with grey flecks covering his shoulders, flanks and legs. Me and Jon stood and stared as the wind rattled the door and rushed through the gaps in the old stone walls.

I wanted to tell him that it was fantastic. That it was brilliant and magnificent. I wanted to tell him that it was the best thing he'd ever done, that he was a genius. I didn't say any of these things. In the end all I managed was, 'It's bloody ace.' Jon pushed past me, all fear lost, and stood underneath the horse's head and looked up and said, 'It bloody is', and my dad stood with a big, proud grin on his face and nodded. He knew that we were right.

We all walked around him and looked from different angles. We stroked him and patted him, ran our hands down his legs and across his chest and slapped him and prodded him. Jon leant forward and nervously sniffed him. And then we stood back and stood still and just looked.

Eventually Dad told us we should get back to the house. He went around the room and blew out the candles and covered the carving back up. He locked the door behind us and we trooped to the kitchen. Dad made us tea and toast and told us he was going to start taking it to the forest as soon as he got chance. He looked relaxed. He looked like he had finished a tough job and finished it well. We spoke about how good it would look and how shocked people would be when they found him, rearing up on his hind legs, miles from anywhere, deep in the trees. I could see people approaching cautiously, gently touching him like we had done, and then laughing and looking around for a clue: who had put him there and why? And then, when they found nothing, they would shake their heads and reluctantly carry on their walk. Leaving the carving behind and looking over their shoulder as they headed out of the clearing and back into the gloom and darkness of the forest. Checking that he really is there, that they really had just stumbled across a massive wooden horse deep in the middle of nowhere.

Jon stayed late, even though it was school the next day. We talked about possible future plans and future carvings, and then, when Jon couldn't keep his eyes open any longer, we drove him home down the fell lane. Because it was so dark Dad insisted on taking Jon to the end of the lane, to his doorstep, and as we approached the car headlights lit up the house, illuminating the junk in the front yard and the newspaper-covered windows – the shabbiness. Jon jumped out as soon as the car pulled to a stop and shot around the back of the house. Dad stayed put with the engine ticking over and the headlights shining. 'Jon lives here?' he asked.

I nodded and said, 'With his grandparents.'

'Jesus,' Dad said, 'It's worse than our place.'

He turned the car around and we drove back up the lane. As we travelled up the steep track the headlights shone out across the fields and lit them a bed-sheet white and I looked up at the sky. The stars glinted like pin heads in the black sky and I thought it impossible that they were burning suns. Dad followed my eyes and when we got out of the car we both stood and stared up into the cold sky for ages until my teeth started to chatter and I couldn't hide it any more and Dad laughed and dragged me inside.

And then the letter came

My life changed the split second Brian Stuart's lorry shattered Mum's car. Everything previous to that moment is before and everything else is after. The walk home is a strange limbo time but if I had to choose I would put it in the after category. Everything had changed; it's just that I hadn't been told. When I think about myself walking the hour-long walk home I'm furious with that person for not knowing, for not working it out somehow. For not knowing that everything had changed. But there was no way I could know until I walked into our house to see my dad sitting in his chair with a look on his face that I will never forget. There was no warning shot and there were no sirens. There should have been a sign painted across the sky telling me my life had changed for ever. But there was nothing. The flowers still stood in the garden and my key still fitted the lock. I walked down the hallway, like I had done a thousand times before, only this time every step took me closer to the end of my old life and the start of a new one that I didn't want. I didn't learn from this though. It didn't teach me anything. I thought that was my big moment, my life's tragedy, and I got sloppy and I relaxed and I wasn't prepared when I should have been.

I was home from school and I threw my bag down in the kitchen as usual and idly picked up the letter that was left lying on the corner of the table and read that *new information has come to light and due to this information available to us we need to re-examine the records and statements and see if we arrive at the same conclusions*. I read that they would need to speak to Mr Gerald Redridge and a meeting had been arranged for Wednesday the 15th at 11 a.m. I read that they did understand that this would be upsetting for all parties concerned and they apologised for this upset caused. They hoped that he understood that they were trying to establish the facts of the tragic road-traffic accident that occurred on Crofts Bank Road on April the 11th of this year. They said that another inquest would be held at a date yet to be decided. I didn't understand. What was to be investigated? What new information and how did it matter? She was dead. Brian Stuart was dead. There was nothing left to investigate.

And then I thought of my dad. He would have got home from dropping me at school at around 8.45 as usual. The letter would have probably been waiting in the hallway and he normally opened the post before he went to his workroom. I counted the hours in my head: one two three four five six seven hours and ten minutes since he'd read it. I listened carefully to the house. It sounded empty.

I tried to be hopeful; I checked the workroom first. It hadn't been unlocked. I walked back to the house, heading for his bedroom. I didn't rush. His bedroom door was open and I could see him from the landing – I could see the lower half of his legs lying stock still on the bed. Shoes still on. I took a deep breath and walked two steps into the room. He was lying face down, spread-eagled on the bed, arms hanging over the sides. The room smelt of whisky and damp. I walked over to the bed and sat down on the edge, next to his head. His back rose and fell an inch. I was about to walk away, to let him sleep it off, when he turned to me and said, 'Hello, Luke.' He put his arm around my neck and pulled me down to the bed and we lay side by side. The room darkened quickly and he fell asleep.

It was midnight. We were sat at the kitchen table. We

both had a coffee. He was explaining. 'Your mum had stopped taking the lithium.' He blinked and looked at me.

'So?'

'Well, the lithium kept her stable, didn't it?'

'It kept her quiet,' I said.

He nodded. 'It did, but it also controlled the highs and lows, didn't it? When she was on the lithium she was never manic and she never . . .'

He smiled and shook his head and said, 'Crashed.'

I asked if he'd known that she'd stopped taking the pills but he shook his head.

'It's only come out now. Dr Hanson was on leave at the time of the accident and the inquest, but when he came back he heard about it all, and checked his files and found out that your mum hadn't picked up her prescription for a couple of weeks before the accident.'

'So what are they thinking?' I asked. I knew what they were thinking. But I wanted him to say it, so the words were spoken and out and in the air. I wanted to hear exactly what they sounded like, to experience their journey from his mouth to my ear.

He sighed and said, 'They think that if she'd stopped taking the lithium, she may have been depressed, and if she was depressed she may have caused the crash deliberately.'

I said it. 'They think it was suicide.'

My dad nodded.

'Yes, they think it might be suicide.'

I didn't think it was suicide. I knew it wasn't. She might have stopped taking the lithium but she wasn't depressed. I could spot the signs of depression. They were obvious to me. Dad had lived with it longer and it was instinctive to him. He could tell by the way she walked in a room or he would notice the tension across her back as she filled the kettle. He would see that she was wearing a top with a stain on the right sleeve two days on the run and he would know it was back. We had seen depression. We had seen her in bed, white and thin and clinging hard to the sheets. We had worried and fussed and been told to go away, to leave her alone. So we had sat downstairs and looked up at the ceiling and stopped on the stairs and watched the closed bedroom door and listened for a sign that she was coming out of the blackness. Silence was bad. And it could last for days. Any sound was good – the sound of the shower, the sound of wardrobe doors being opened. It didn't matter what, it meant she was moving, it meant she had won again.

But she wasn't depressed the day she died. The morning of the crash had been a normal 'good' morning. I came down to the kitchen, late as usual. Mum made me eat some cereal, which turned soggy before I got halfway through it. She told me not to forget my art folder and then flapped and hurried me into the car. Dad came out of his workroom with a cup of coffee and waved us both off. Mum sang along to a rubbish song on the radio and I pretended I was embarrassed.

She checked I had my lunch money and kissed me before I climbed out of the car. As I walked away I saw her lean forward and turn the radio back up and she waved goodbye, mouthing she would pick me up later, blew me a kiss and drove off, waving as she went. There wasn't a drop of depression anywhere near her that day.

But, of course, the police didn't know any of that. The only facts they had were that Megan Redridge was in a massive car crash and died. And that Megan Redridge suffered from bipolar disorder and had stopped taking her medication at least two weeks before the crash. They also knew that both vehicles involved were tested and neither had any discernible faults. And they needed to know which file to put my mum's death in: Accident or Suicide.

P.P.P.P.P.Painting

Painting helped. If I look back I can see that even when my mum was alive I painted more when things were looking bad. When the storm clouds gathered around her and she started spinning out of control, I painted. In the aftermath – the long, dark, quiet days, when she was locked away in her room – I painted. I painted and drew during better days too, when everything was settled and calm, but it wasn't as focused. It didn't drain my energy and absorb my thoughts like it sometimes did. And to be honest, the work, well, it wasn't as good. It lacked tension I suppose.

Since we'd moved to Duerdale I'd done nothing much

but paint. I was more consistent these days too and more often than not the paintings developed as I expected and wanted them to. At times it felt like I was in complete control of shade, shadow and line. And it felt good. When it's going well, it's both an intense and a calm experience at the same time. It's exciting. It's surprising how quickly you can ruin a painting though. One minute it's all going down exactly as it should and the next, you've gone too far and can't get it back. The trick is not to get too excited, even when things are going well. My dad told me that when carving or painting you have to take charge, that there has always got to be an element of control. And he's right. People have this idea that an artist can be wild and abandoned and fling the paint on the canvas and throw it around like it doesn't matter. Well, you can be confident and bold, but you have to take responsibility, you have to take care. You can't be hasty or dismissive or it will show in the finished painting. It will look rushed and somehow, in some way, it won't look right. I've found that what works for me is to try and trick myself into thinking that I'm not really there. I imagine that it isn't my arm or my hand. I imagine that I'm watching someone else mix the paint together and if the painting is emerging as it should, then I try to remove myself from the process as much as possible.

I had moved on from painting the cairn at the top of Bowland Fell, but the fell was still my main hunting ground. I painted wind-blasted trees, abandoned derelict barns and ice-cold, slate-grey streams. And all these paintings had one constant. They were all filled with the strange light I'd only ever found on top of Bowland Fell. It cast the tree as a suspicious silhouette against the sky and it twinkled threateningly in the breath-stealing cold water of the streams. Even on the increasingly rare warmer days there was a hint of menace in the light up there. It changed in a second, sometimes almost disappearing, and what minutes before had been a clear view of leafless trees and long, low, dry-stone walls would suddenly become dark and murky and abstract. The light on Bowland Fell lit things in a brutal, fascinating way and added drama to each painting. I told my dad about it and he nodded and said, 'That's northern light', and even though we had only moved an hour further north I think he was right; it was a different light. My room was almost full of finished canvases and I had to store some in the workroom alongside Dad's carvings. He helped me take them down and hang them on the walls and when we were finished he looked around him and said, 'You're good at this, you know.' I tried not to let him see me grinning.

I had less luck at DHS. I asked my floral-frocked art teacher, Mrs Richmond, when I could do some painting. She replied that this term we were concentrating on ceramics. I said that she misunderstood – I wanted to know when I could go to the art room outside of lessons to paint. She eyed me suspiciously, as if I was intent on causing trouble. She told me the art room was kept locked when there wasn't a teacher present. I asked if I was able to paint after school, but she was starting to get impatient now. She told me that there was no need to worry, that for the last ten years she'd managed to teach the whole syllabus in the allotted class hours. She said I wouldn't miss out on anything. I gave up. I decided I would stick to Bowland Fell and its menacing light. She could keep her dingy art room.

Well-being

They were pinpoint attacks. They happened in dark corners of quiet corridors. Always when no one else was around. Always finished with a spit in the face. Jon said the knife was never used, but he was shown it a couple of times. Just so he knew: this is what is happening; this is what could happen. The shoves and kicks and slaps I saw in the corridor didn't even register any more with Jon. They were just passing storm clouds and they happened all the time. Kieran Judd was the nightmare in dark corners with the knife settled in his pocket, sunk into the shadows, his fists and feet itching. Jon tried to shrug it away, as if it was a part of life, like headaches and homework. And it was clear why. The attempted visits from the Social Services were happening almost daily now so Jon treated this stuff as an inconvenience, a fly to be swatted away. Letters were being hand-delivered and Jon had started opening them. They would be coming, the letters said. With or without agreement. To speak to Mr and Mrs Mansfield, to speak to Jon Mansfield. To assess their well-being.

Jon carried on, head down, putting up no resistance to Judd's feet and fists. I'd seen kids at my old school crumble under less. It was different there though, they were serious and there was a message: BULLYING IN

ANY FORM WILL NOT BE TOLERATED. They even stopped using the word *bullying* and used words you normally only hear on the news or in police dramas: *harassment, persecution, assault, attack*.

This all happened after Liam Dewhurst, a boy with a speech impediment, was bullied so much that he swallowed half a bottle of pills and had to be rushed to hospital to have his stomach pumped. He'd left a note and named names and it was on the local news and in the local paper. His parents were interviewed and there was a photograph on the front page where they looked upset, angry and defiant all at the same time. They said that they'd tried to approach the school but had been told that it was in hand, that it was being dealt with. They said that they'd done what they could but the school didn't want to know. The school had sent them away when they needed help. Liam's mum said that if her son had died the school would've had blood on its hands. That was the line the paper used as the headline.

The next day the school rocket-launched itself into action. The police were called and kids expelled and excluded. The headmaster gave an assembly in front of the whole school. An angry address. Teachers lined the hall walls, arms folded and grim-faced. None of them warmed their hands on their usual cups of coffee. They stood straight-backed and silent. The headmaster stalked down the hall, from the oldest kids at the back to the youngest at the front, his head high, his face concrete. Each footstep echoed with intent. When he was in front of the microphone he didn't speak for a while, just shuffled some papers, taking his time, thinking things through. Eventually he looked out over the lines of children, methodically taking in each and every face. Looking for a reaction. He began with his voice a whisper, his tone thin. Later he occasionally leapt to a roar only to drop back down again. It didn't matter: everybody heard every word regardless of volume. And everybody felt guilty. Even the good kids. He spoke about cowardice, lack of honour, cruelty and consequence. He said that it would not happen in one of his schools. Ever. Again. In all his years in the teaching profession he said, he had never been angrier than he was right now. And everyone believed him. When we all trooped out, forty minutes later, exhausted and silent, I saw that some of the faces of the kids from the year below mine were smeared and mucky with tears, eyes red and puffed. Even some of the older children looked pale. As we left the hall nobody pushed and shoved and mucked about, we just filed out quietly, the way the teachers wanted us to every day.

It struck me that Duerdale High was less concerned with bullying as an issue. Maybe because it had yet to have a suicide attempt and the local camera crews camped outside. The way Jon was treated would never have happened at my old school. Kids shouted out 'Slack Jaw!' as they passed him on the corridor. And I saw teachers smile, in on the joke, just a bit of fun, no real harm. But if that happened when they were there, what did they think happened when they weren't?

It was only when we were getting changed for PE one afternoon that I realised how serious it was. We were stood facing the changing-room wall, reluctantly getting ready, and Jon had taken his shirt off. As he raised his arms to hang it on the peg I saw a rainbow of colour flash in the air. I turned to look and made him hold his skinny arms out towards me. They were covered in bruises, all running into and over each other.

It wasn't as if I was the only person who could see them. There were at least thirty of us in that room, but nobody else reacted. And why would they? It was Slack Jaw. The weird granddad-looking kid from the fell. The kid who hid in the Library all the time. The one who couldn't catch or kick a ball. The one that everyone said stank of piss. (He didn't.) And what did he expect anyway? Dressing like that and looking like that? It was inevitable.

Later that lunchtime we were in Duerdale Library. Jon was sat at his usual desk and I was opposite, pretending to read. We had a conversation that quickly escalated from hissed whispers to loud voices and one of the librarians had to look over and shout that we would be out if we carried on. Jon looked at me as if that signalled his final and winning point: No, he did not want to talk about Kieran Judd. No, he did not want me to do anything about Kieran Judd and would I please shut up about the whole fucking thing and let him read his book. I stormed out, banging the door behind me, the noise exploding through the stuffy calm of the Library. I left him in the safe, warm silence with his stupid, frustrating, bloody head buried in a battered copy of *Amazing Facts about the World in which You Live*.

I knew why I was so angry. I wanted to make amends for what happened with Peter Corkland. Peter was a boy at my old school and his life was hell and one day I made it worse. Even after they clamped down on bullying, little changed for Peter. He was the fattest boy in school, the fattest boy in town, and everyone called him Peter the Pie Man. It's not cruel to describe him as fat though; it's just the truth. He was massive. Every part of him was big, even his wrists and ankles. They looked like they belonged to a fat baby, flesh rolling over itself at the joints. He had his own special chair in the classroom because the standard chairs might not be safe. There were only a couple of these chairs in the school and somebody had to make sure that one of them would be in his next lesson. Normally a teacher got one of the other kids to take one because it would take Peter too long to carry it.

He used to wear his dad's old clothes to school and it was a strange sight until you got used to it. There he was, twice as wide as any of us, in his dad's shirt and trousers looking ready for the office, but with his school bag slung over his shoulder. He didn't wear a blazer because they just didn't make them that big. He wasn't allowed to do sport with us; the teachers wouldn't risk it. They were worried he would collapse and die or something so they just made him walk around the playing field while we played football or did athletics.

He eventually got diagnosed with Prader Willi Syndrome, which meant he ate too much, but it wasn't his fault. He never felt full, even after a big meal. One of our teachers said that trying to stop Peter eating was like trying to stop ice melt in the midday sun. And it was a bit mean the way he said it in front of everyone, but it was true. Sometimes people give excuses for why they are fat. They say it's because of water retention, glands, big bones or a thyroid problem, things like that. And nobody really believes them. But Peter did have a reason, there was an excuse, but he never bothered to explain, he never used his illness as a reason for his size. Maybe he couldn't see the point, couldn't see that it would change anything.

He was always eating. On the way to school he would eat crisps from his left pocket and take swigs from the drink in his right pocket. He kept his chocolate in his school bag. He stashed food in his desk at school and ate during lessons. Nobody else was allowed but the teachers gave up trying to stop Peter. He seemed a nice guy really, but he was a bit shy I think, and I never really got to know him. I had my few friends and my drawing and we just never seemed to be in the same place at the same time. And I suppose it's hard to be friends with someone who has to stop and rest when walking from one class to the next, someone who can never join in with any games or sport because he gets too tired. It didn't bother me that he was fat though; I never had a problem with him at all. I was never one of the ones who called him the Pie Man or threw food at him in the canteen. Like I said, my family welcomed outsiders. That's what makes what happened worse.

It was lunchtime and it was pouring down and it had

been raining all day. This meant that the art room was packed. I was here every lunch but on wet days they opened it up to everyone. I hated it like that. People just mucked around and shoved each other about and flirted and argued and you could never get anything done. There were loads of us sat round a big table but only a couple of us were drawing, everyone else was just bored and wishing they could be outside. Some of the boys were a couple of years older than me and my friends. I didn't know any of their names and they were loud and looking for people to pick on. I was keeping my head down. Just drawing. After a few minutes I could sense one of them was stood behind me, looking. I thought he was going to take the mick, grab my drawing off me, make me plead for it back, that kind of thing. Instead he said, 'That's brilliant, that's really good. That's him, isn't it?' He pointed at my friend, Ian, who was sat opposite me. I nodded. One of the other older boys came round and had a look too. He said that nobody in his year could draw like that. They seemed really impressed. I won't lie; I was proud, it felt good.

Just then one of the older lads shouted, 'Look at the Pie Man!' People ran to the window and watched Peter below, out in the rain, walking slowly towards the school with rain running down his face and dripping off his nose and chin. He seemed oblivious to the weather. He stopped every now and again and leant on a wall to get his breath. As he got closer some of the boys banged on the window and chanted, 'Pie Man! Pie Man! Pie Man!' But he didn't look up; he was very good at ignoring people, and they got bored and things quietened down. I carried on trying to finish my drawing before the bell for the next lesson went. The room fell silent for a few minutes and it was good; it was like it normally was. As I was concentrating on getting Ian's hair right, spikes in all the right places, I felt somebody's eyes on me. I looked up and saw the older boy who had complimented my drawing looking at me with a glint in his eye and a smile on his face. He leaned forward. 'Do you know what? You should draw the Pie Man . . .' There was a second's silence and then, suddenly, that's what the whole room was saying. 'Yeah, draw him. It'll be brilliant . . .'; 'Come on, just do it quickly, draw him . . .'; 'Get him some more paper. Give him some room . . .'; 'Shut up, let him get on with it . . .'

I had never been the centre of attention before and I never want to be again. And I didn't want to draw Peter. I really didn't. The shouting didn't stop though, and they were all crowded around me, waiting for the picture, telling me how brilliant it would be. I tried to stand up to leave but I got pushed back down. I quickly drew a picture where Peter wasn't half as fat as he really was. They ripped that up and started getting annoyed. I got a shove to my head. I felt a fist in my back. They knew I could do it well.

I tried to get it over with quickly. I did it fast, in a couple of minutes. A quick, horrible caricature. As I drew somebody shouted, 'Show him eating!' So I put the drink bottle in one pocket, the crisps in another, and a hand full of food going up to his open mouth. Crumbs everywhere. It was finished. It was horrible. I wanted to rip it up. One of the older boys shouted 'Brilliant!' Tore it off me and ran out of the room followed by his mates.

My drawing was photocopied and pinned up on classroom boards and handed out to kids as they walked between lessons. Someone had written, 'The Pie Man!' across the top before it was copied, just in case anyone was too stupid to tell who it was. Before long people were sending it from phone to phone. It wasn't long until the teachers saw it and I got dragged in front of the headmaster. And not long till they called my mum and dad.

My mum couldn't believe it. She'd never been so angry and upset with me. She could barely look at me and she couldn't look at the drawing. When the head-master pushed it in front of her she ripped it up. When we got home she said she didn't like me right now, and asked me to leave her alone. I tried to apologise but she didn't want to hear it and Dad told me that I needed to give her some time, that I needed to let her calm down. And anyway, I didn't know how to explain. What could I say? 'It wasn't me. I didn't want to do it. I just wanted them to go away.' It sounded pathetic and it just didn't sound true. How could I be made to draw a picture? I don't know if she ever really forgave me properly. Things weren't right for days after that and I wish I'd never drawn it and I was sorry that I was cruel to Peter. He never said anything though. I think he just thought it was the kind of thing that would always happen to him. There didn't seem anything I could do to make things right and it still upsets me sometimes, even now.

It makes me angry that she knew that I did that before she died and that I never really managed to explain how it had happened.

I should have just let them beat me up. That would have been much better.

Bad backs and sore arms

It was harder than he thought it would be. I could tell after the first day. When he drove me and Jon to school the back of the car was already loaded with the first piece of the carving to be taken to the clearing. He said he would start off slowly, start off easy, so he took one of the lighter sections to carry. He arrived back at the house just as I returned home from school and climbed out of the car a different man. There was mud streaked across his face and his shirt was dirty. He walked slowly, bent over like a flamingo's neck. 'You all right?' I asked. 'Kind of,' he replied. 'A bit tired, that's all.' He shuffled passed me, through the front door and into the kitchen and lowered himself into his chair with a grimace on his face. He was asleep before the kettle boiled.

The next few days followed a similar pattern. And every time he returned to the house I thought that would be it. That he would admit defeat, say it was too hard, a bloody stupid idea and let's please not mention the stupid bloody wooden horse again. I expected the whisky bottle to come out and a toast to knocking the whole thing on the bloody head. The whisky bottle did come out, and he had a drink, but I was watching closely and he wasn't drinking like he did when we first arrived in Duerdale, when a bottle could disappear in a night. After a few more days, I noticed the slightest changes. He was still as tired when he got home, but in the mornings, even though he complained and moaned about the pains in his bones and joints and hobbled about like an old man, he seemed a little brighter and stronger despite all of this. He didn't look as fragile as eggshell any more. A few days after this change I noticed a muscle in his arm that flickered as he stirred his coffee. I hadn't seen that before. There was even the slightest touch of colour to his cheeks, a thin veil of red resting on the grey. He was still as skinny as ever but it seemed less of a hospital bed thin, less of a dangerous thin. I thought to myself that I must be imaging things, that a few days dragging lumps of wood through a forest couldn't change a man much surely? But each time I risked a glance, I could clearly see that he was ever so slightly starting to look healthier.

I offered to help with moving the carving but he said that there was nothing I could really help with and I knew that he was right. I'd tried to lift some of the pieces in the workroom and I could do, just. But it would have been impossible for me to move them further than the car outside, never mind all the way through the forest. Each morning when Jon clambered into the car he looked in the back to see what parts were being transported that day. He would see that it was one of the flanks or thighs and say, 'Whoa! That's a big piece, that must kill you!' And Dad would say, 'Yes, Jon, it might just about do that.' And we would wish him luck as we climbed out of the car and said goodbye and he would drive off with a look in his eye that made you think he might be going to war.

Unexpected speed

I always thought that organisations like Social Services moved slowly. That they crept along precariously like a mobile home being moved on a motorway. That isn't always the case. Duerdale Social Services could lumber forward as fast as an angry rhinoceros when it wanted to. Mr McGrath and Ms Green turned up with a signed order from the Family Court saying they had a right to inspect the premises. And they brought a policeman. Just in case either grandparent miraculously rose from their chair, grew strength and power into their thinning, shrinking bones and wrestled the social workers to the floor.

Jon was at school when they arrived. The first he knew about it was when he turned the corner in the lane and saw his grandma being wheeled into an ambulance with a look of astonishment on her face. His granddad was next and he gave more resistance but there was no power in the swats he aimed at the ambulance men. It was as futile as a man falling off a cliff trying to air-grab his way back to safety. Jon ran forward down the lane as fast as he could towards the ambulance, police car and social workers when he should have really turned and run the other way. He was put in the police car and all three vehicles travelled in a convoy to Duerdale Hospital. The policeman told him not to worry, that he wasn't being arrested, but Jon said he did do that 'pushing your head down thing', so it can't be bumped on the car roof and you can't sue for assault later.

I only learnt all this when the phone rang that night. That was unusual in itself and I was already half expecting some kind of trouble before Dad called me down from my room to the chilly hallway. He passed me the phone and mouthed, 'Jon.' He sensed that something wasn't right too; he lingered by the open kitchen door, his shadow falling out into the hall as he pretended to dry the dishes.

I sat on the stairs, and said, 'Hello?' There was no reply, just the hum of the phone line. Then I heard the sound of footsteps squeaking on hard floor. I was trying to work out where he could be when he spoke.

'I'm at the hospital.'

'Hospital?'

He told me about turning the corner in the lane, about Mr McGrath and Ms Green, his grandma's bewilderment, and his granddad's resistance. He told me about the policeman's hand on his head and the convoy to the hospital. He told me that he was being kept in, that they were doing tests to see if he was malnourished or vitamin deficient or something. They said they wanted to establish his 'general level of health'. They'd checked his height, checked his weight, checked his body mass index, he said. They'd shone lights in his eyes, lights in his ears, lights in his mouth, lights up his nose. They'd listened to his chest from front and back. They'd rooted through his hair and peered at his scalp. They'd smiled fixed smiles at him and spoken in singsong voices. They were too kind, too gentle with him, he said. Like he might be made of breadcrumbs. Like part of him might just fall off. Then they found the bruises on his arms. It was like they'd got home and found a smashed window and their faces turned hard and their note-taking increased. Jon saw what was going on and told them that his grandparents hadn't done that. They had never done anything like that. A nurse told him not to worry; they weren't suggesting that they had. He should just try and rest. He needed to rest and worrying wasn't resting, was it? He said that they wouldn't or couldn't answer the question he kept asking, 'When can we go home?'

He'd fallen silent now and I wasn't sure what to say. I tried to cheer him up and told him that after living in that house for so long, he would be immune to anything, immune to death even. He didn't say anything. I looked at the time on my watch and saw that it was still early. I would give it a go. I asked him what ward he was on and told him not to worry, I would try and see him soon. I hung up and shouted for Dad.

Coloured lines on shiny floors

Everybody says they hate hospitals. I don't. At least if you make it to a hospital you stand a chance of coming back out. I know there are people dying and people in pain. People sitting at the edges of beds watching and wishing that they could help. Making deals in their head with a God they haven't thought about for years, thinking, take me instead, please. But there are also people getting better and people getting good news. There are people who had given up hope being handed a second chance and thinking, this time I won't squander it. This time I will savour every hour and every day. And maybe, at least for the next few weeks, they will and the world will look precious and new to them again. So, no, I don't hate hospitals. I would have given anything to have been able to visit my mum in hospital after the crash. To see her lying in bed, a weak smile on her face, a leg in plaster, and covered in bruises, would have made me the happiest person in the world. Of course I hate the smell. Hospital smell is horrible. A warm sickly scent. Everyone hates that. It always feels good to get back outside and take a deep breath of fresh air and shake the hospital odour from your clothes.

We arrived just as evening visiting time had begun and the corridors were teeming with people carrying flowers, cards and magazines and books. Some looked like regulars; they strode confidently ahead, not checking signs, impatient to reach their destination. Others were more like us: unsure and hesitant, clearly the new boys. We stood staring for ages at the huge board in the hospital foyer, looking for Bowland Ward. We eventually found out that Bowland Ward was a green-zone ward and that to reach it we needed to follow the green-line path. I didn't understand. And then Dad pointed at the different coloured lines that criss-crossed along the shiny and scuffed floors. As we walked Dad asked why Jon was here and what was going on. I acted dumb and shrugged and muttered nothings. I didn't know how much Jon wanted anyone to know anything. And it wasn't up to me to tell anyone anything. The green line led us through a maze of corridors and past departments with names that I could barely pronounce. It took us from one grey building to another and in and out of big silver lifts and further and further into the belly of the hospital. And just when I was worried that we were about to end up at the outskirts of our old town we turned a corner and saw Bowland Ward lurking at the end of the corridor.

We approached slowly and pushed our faces up against the window, and in the far corner of the furthest flung ward of Duerdale Royal Infirmary we found Jon. Tucked up in bed, looking even younger than normal. We pushed the doors open and Jon glanced up at the noise. When he saw us, a cheek-bursting smile spread across his face. I swear it would have broken the heart of even Kieran Judd.

We had to pass four other beds to get to him. Four beds containing sickly-looking men, coughing and spluttering, moaning about the heat. One saying he could murder a pint, one gasping for a fag. They chuckled amongst themselves. We reached Jon and followed the usual hospital rituals: finding chairs, working out who sits where, and then, when finally settled, the awkward silence when you realise the whole world is going to hear your conversation. Dad took the lead. He leant forward and gently asked, 'How are you doing, Jon?'

Jon smiled again. 'Good, good, thanks. I'm OK.'

A couple of seconds of silence followed.

'I just don't know what's going to happen next, they won't tell me anything.'

'Why are you in *here*?' I asked, nodding towards the men.

'They've run out of beds in the children's ward and I was the oldest so they put me in here. This lot are nice though.'

Jon nodded over to his ward mates and me and Dad turned round. All four smiled and waved at us. We waved back.

'Don't worry,' the man in the nearest bed said. 'We'll look after him.'

Dad smiled and said thanks.

'You the father, are you?' he asked.

Dad shook his head and said no, he wasn't. There was an awkward pause but then the man continued, 'Well, like I said, nothing to worry about, we'll see that he's OK.'

The men started chatting amongst themselves again and Dad turned back to Jon. He clapped his hands together and said, 'So . . .', and he looked like he was about to ask a question, but he came to a halt, with his hands clasped together in mid-air and his mouth closed around the word 'so'. He looked like a devout man offering up prayer but nothing else came out, nothing else happened. It was just Dad and a brick wall. And I think that was quite a moment for him. A camera-flash moment when he realised that he'd no idea how he'd ended up here. At the hospital bedside of a thirteen-year-old boy he hardly knew, in a town he didn't know existed a few months earlier. I think it might have been then, in the white light of a hospital ward on a winter night, when he finally understood how fully the fog had descended over the last few months. He looked startled. His mouth opened and closed gormlessly a few times. He looked from Jon to me and back to me again and said, 'Who's going to fill me in then?'

Latvia

We were both silent. And then Jon said, 'Tell him.' I asked if he was sure, and he nodded that he was. He looked exhausted. He looked too tired to handle the coughs that kept hacking at his chest. He seemed happy to let me paint the whole gruesome picture and just occasionally nod that I was speaking the truth when Dad looked to him for confirmation, thinking that I must be exaggerating a little least. I didn't exaggerate because I didn't need to. I just described the house as I remembered it with the rubbish, and the smell and the black scurrying creatures that I didn't fully see and didn't dare ask if they were mice or rats. I described the cats, the newspaper mountains and Jon's grandparents, rocking themselves, insane in their old and stained bedclothes. I hoped I wasn't embarrassing Jon but I saw this as his apples-and-oranges incident and our chance to get everything out in the open. And anyway, he looked too tired to be embarrassed.

When I finished Dad was quiet for a few seconds and then he shook his head and said that he was sorry. He should have seen that something wasn't right. But Jon and me said, no, he couldn't have known, it was a secret that we wanted to keep. And we all knew that whilst this was true it was also true that at times during the last few months a hurricane could have lifted our house up off the ground, spun it around in space and landed it in Latvia, and Dad probably wouldn't have noticed, would have just opened another bottle and poured another glass when the dust settled and the windows stopped shaking.

Dad asked questions: How long had it been like this? What did they do for money? Did they get any help or benefits? And again: Why hadn't we told him? Eventually he ran himself quiet and he saw that Jon was finding it hard to keep up with all the questions anyway. A nurse appeared on the ward and seemed surprised to see us. She told us that visiting hours had finished half an hour ago and we would have to leave. As I put the chairs back and grabbed our coats Dad asked who he could contact, who was the doctor. The nurse gave him the name and told him to ring the hospital in the morning. Before we left I asked her what was going to happen to Jon and she said she didn't know but that she was pretty sure that he wouldn't be going anywhere for a few days at least. Jon seemed to relax a little at this news and he started to give in to the tiredness. He just managed to stay awake as we said our goodbyes although his eyes were fluttering with sleep before we got our coats on.

Black roads

We left the hospital and headed for the car. It was easy

to spot, the car park had emptied quickly and ours was almost the only vehicle left. Dad, as usual, had parked in the most remote corner he could find and we walked across the brightly lit tarmac with the hum of the hospital fading behind us. Within a few minutes we were a world away from the shiny white wards and metal machines and nurses dressed in blue and were rolling along on black country lanes, trees on either side and darkness all around. I had only recently understood that night does not always mean blackness, that on some nights the moon will illuminate the fields and trees and roads like a floodlight. Even on the fell, without any streetlights for miles around, on certain nights you could walk along tracks with no torch needed, the light from the moon bright enough to guide you. Other nights, nights when the moon hid or was covered by cloud, it felt like a medieval darkness descended on the valley. It was a blackness that swallowed torchlight whole three steps out from the front door. Tonight was a black night and the only light for miles around came from our weak headlights which only just cut through the thick dark. We were halfway home when Dad cleared his throat and it might as well have been a drum roll. He was about to break his car silence and I braced myself. He spoke faster than usual, his voice hard with determination, three short sentences, pushed out into the car like gunfire.

'It's the inquest. Soon. They've set a date.'

I didn't respond; I could tell more would be coming. He leant forward in his seat. He told me that they'd spoken to everyone else involved, they just needed to speak to him now and had gone ahead and set a date for the official inquest.

'Are you going to be OK? With what people might say? The implications?'

I thought about his questions but I didn't need to think too long. I'd been thinking about the inquest since the day the letter arrived and I knew exactly how I felt. So I told him that I wasn't really interested in what they had to say. He shot me a surprised look and I explained. I told him, I *knew* it was an accident, that Mum wasn't depressed that day and it didn't matter to me what anyone else said, particularly a group of people who had never even met her. He looked across at me again to see that I was being honest, to check that I wasn't trying to fob him off, but he could see I was telling the truth. He nodded, he seemed pleased, and said that was good, that he had come to the same conclusion himself. He was sorry that it was all being dragged up again, he said, and he was sorry that Brian Stuart's family might be thinking Mum was to blame, but there was nothing we could do to change anything. He said that as long as we knew what we thought, that was what was important.

We drove on in silence for a couple of minutes before he spoke again. He said that as long as I was doing all right, getting by, that was the main thing. He looked to me for a response so I shrugged and said I supposed I was OK, that compared to Jon right now I was pretty much King of the Castle. Then he asked if I knew that I could always talk to him about anything, no matter what, including Mum. A river burst its banks in my chest. I squinted and stared ahead. I dug my nails into the palm of my hand until it stung. I wasn't going to cry. I gathered myself. I nodded and said, yes and thanks, I did know that but thanks.

I didn't know that at all. I tried not to think about all the times I wanted to ask him questions, to talk about her, to remember her out loud. I remember wanting to ask where all her clothes were and where all her little bottles of nail varnish had got to. Had he boxed all her belongings and brought them with us? Where was the book she had started and never finished? Was all that stuff left unpacked in one of the dirty spare bedrooms with all the other boxes we hadn't opened? I wanted to know if he ever blamed Brian Stuart for driving such a stupidly big lorry that left her without a chance. I wanted to know if he was ever angry with her for crashing, for maybe losing concentration, just for a second. And I wanted to ask if he ever blamed me. If he blamed me for having a stupid after-school art club that meant I couldn't get the school bus home and had to be picked up. But I didn't ask anything. It was enough that he'd mentioned her; that her name was back in circulation.

Dad relaxed, he sank into his seat and his shoulders dropped. He talked about the inquest. He told me that they would look at all the evidence again and take Mum's mental state and medication into consideration and then come to a final conclusion about whether her death was an accident, suicide or would be left as an open verdict. I nodded and said I understood. I didn't say so but the whole thing seemed as useless as a machine designed to test the wetness of water. We turned off the fell road and onto our track and were bumping along as usual when Dad braked suddenly. We stopped in almost exactly the same spot we'd nearly killed Jon on our first day in Duerdale and I peered out into the dark to see why. The biggest owl I'd ever seen was sat on a gatepost by the side of the road. He was tall and white with big black eyes. He seemed oblivious to us but when Dad turned the car engine off he turned his head our way and looked right at us, his eyes taking in everything. He watched us for a while and then, bored, turned his gaze past the car and back down the road. Dad turned the key in the ignition and we slowly moved off.

I kicked a boy

It was the day after the hospital visit and I was feeling frazzled. I was sat in an empty classroom working on my Maths homework. I hate Maths. My old Maths teacher, Mr Knowles, told me that Maths is the most logical subject of them all. That all you have to do is follow rules and formulas and you can't go wrong. He said that if you had enough time you could teach a monkey Maths. That made me hate it even more. We had to answer from 17a to 29b before the next lesson. The next lesson was in ten minutes and I was stuck on 17b. I couldn't concentrate and I let my ears settle on the shouts and calls from the playing field. My mind drifted and I remembered something that struck me in the first few days after Mum died. You still get homework. Of course nobody would question it not being done, or it not being done on time for a while at least. But it still gets dished out to everyone, no exceptions. But that was then, at my old school, in the days and weeks after the crash, when the town was still shocked and rallying around and I was still, really, the exception. It was still part of the time when Dad and I would open the front door to find casserole dishes left on the doorstep covered in foil and resting on notes saying things like '40 minutes, gas mark 5. Can be frozen. Sue and Brian xx'.

That was another thing I learnt. When someone dies, people like to cook. Honestly. We couldn't move for food. The freezer was full within two days and in the end Dad had to throw stuff out. Now I'm no longer the exception in the 'no exceptions', I'm just the kid in the empty classroom who hasn't finished his homework and will get into trouble like anyone else.

I lifted my head up towards the ceiling and blinked hard and tried to concentrate on the task in hand. I was about to attempt to refocus on 17b when I saw Kieran Judd and Darren Laycock peering through the classroom window. I looked back down at the page hoping deeply that they would pass along and leave me alone. The door opened a couple of seconds later and they spilt into the room as quickly as water. Kieran Judd pulled out the chair next to me, sat down and folded his arms across his chest. Laycock hung back, sitting on a desktop, waiting for whatever was about to happen to happen. I stared so hard at the question on the page that it started to wobble.

After a few seconds of consideration Judd rocked

back on his chair. He finally spoke. 'So are you and Slack Jaw best mates?' I ignored him and continued staring at question 17b, which might as well have been in Welsh for all the sense I was making of it. Judd continued, 'The thing is, *you* seem all right to me but if you continue hanging around with King . . . Spaz . . . Boy . . .' – he said these words slowly, a gap between each one, cherishing the sound they made – 'then you aren't going to have many other friends are you . . .' It wasn't a question and I remained silent, still staring at the page on my desk, but aware of a strange feeling that had started in my gut. I couldn't place it. It was unfamiliar, but not unpleasant. I tried to ignore Judd, but he didn't want to be ignored and he ploughed on. 'So, are you not bothered about it being just you and Slack Jaw?'

On the word 'jaw' the feeling in my belly exploded. It ran as fast as field mice into my arms and legs and shocked me out of my chair. It robbed me of control and handed it to a mad man and it was terrifying and brilliant. I was stood over Judd before he had chance to move. I grabbed a chunk of his slick straw hair and used it to bang his face down hard on the desk. Before he managed to react I shoved him off his chair and onto the ground. He scrambled to get up and I kicked him hard in the stomach. I made satisfying contact. If he were a football he would've flown.

Laycock didn't know what to do; he was shocked into stillness. Eventually he stirred and made a move forward and I ROARED at him. It came out of my mouth like a train out of a tunnel and I didn't know whose voice it was but I was glad it was there. He looked terrified, like a little boy facing an army. He froze. I told him to fuck off and stand still. He did. I walked over to Judd who was starting to stand up, trying to gather himself to start kicking the hell out of me. I knew he was thinking that he couldn't get beaten up by the artist boy, the boy with the bright green eyes and the spastic friend. But before he could get fully to his feet I charged at him and shoved him against the nearest wall. His head cracked hard against the white tiles, making the sound an egg might. My stomach spun and slipped, a queasiness edging up my throat. I pushed it back down. Our arms were flung around each other and for a few seconds we were hugging more than fighting. I almost had my head in his armpit and I could smell him. New sweat mixing with old sweat. I shoved my body into his and against the wall three times and then held him there. He twisted and tensed and his face turned a royal gala red. A drop of sweat squeezed out and trickled from his temple to the top of his cheek and I wondered if I could make the spots on his forehead pop by pushing harder. I gave it a go and shoved again. I told him that if he ever touched Jon again I would kill him. I asked if he understood. He didn't respond so I pushed harder. I knew that if he didn't answer soon I would cause him harm. His eyes started to water and he squirmed and slithered against the wall, popping like a fish on a boat deck. But I held firm. Eventually he fell slack and nodded. He was scared. I shoved again, one more surge, and then let go. He fell to his hands and knees, gasping for breath. I looked down at him and felt nothing. I glared at Laycock, still daring him to make a move, but he had retreated to a corner. The bell was ringing. I picked up my homework and bag and walked out of the room and straight to my Maths class. At the end of the lesson I handed in my homework. I never did get past 17b though. I got an F.

Skin and bones

Just as I was holding Kieran Judd by his neck and pushing so hard his eyeballs popped, Dad was ringing the hospital and asking to speak to Dr Abdelbaki. He lied and said, yes, he was a close relative, and it was as easy as that. The doctor told him about the tests they had run and the results they had received back.

Jon was, he said, micronutrient malnourished, which was normally referred to as hidden hunger. He said it was more common in the Third World but there were more and more cases of it in Britain and America because of bad diets. He said that it's called hidden hunger because the person may be eating but they are eating the wrong kind of food, food deficient in vitamins and nutrients. The tests showed that Jon didn't have enough iron, vitamin A, zinc or iodine. He was run down and his immune system was weak and as a result he was more prone to catching disease. And when Dad told me that, I thought about the tight, hard, cough that had plagued Jon from the first day he'd turned up at our door and which sometimes grabbed him and shook his chest like an earthquake.

They would keep Jon in hospital for a few days, put

him on a drip and feed him. They would monitor his response and then, if everything went as expected, he should be OK to leave. The doctor asked when Dad would be coming to visit next and told him they would talk more then. Before Dad hung up he asked about the grandparents. And there was a lot to tell but to be blunt they were knackered.

The hospital had run a battery of tests and the doctors were armed with pages of results as evidence. Jon's grandma was suffering from dementia and her mind was gone, her memory dissolved. She didn't know where she was or who her husband was most of the time. Nobody knew what ghosts she could see and when she talked it could just be a name said over and over, or rambling sentences that went nowhere and made no sense. When Jon described her random and fractured speech, it made me think of the book my mum had started to write when she had been unwell. She was troubled by something or everything and when she wasn't sleeping her eyes darted around the room looking for something that wasn't there in the empty corners, a constant expression of worry working her face. The hospital said they would try and make her comfortable but her mental health would only get worse in time. Jon's granddad wasn't as bad. The doctors didn't get much out of him but he knew where he was; he knew what was going on. He just didn't want to talk to anyone about it. He could walk, very slowly, and they were feeding him, trying to make him stronger. Both were as malnourished as Jon and there were no decisions to be made. If they ever did make it out of the hospital, it wouldn't be to go back to their house on the fell. Dad was told it had gone on far too long and things had got out of control. It wouldn't be left to happen again. Jon's grandparents would be found residential care. Jon would be found a home elsewhere. It would, they said, be better for everyone.

I played a trick

I followed Jon's example. I asked Dad if he would give me a lift across town. He looked surprised, I never normally asked to be taken anywhere, but he went to grab the car keys. It was a couple of days after Jon had been admitted to hospital and it was the first night we hadn't been to see him. I could just about remember the way and I made sure we drove past the dark crumbling mills and the breezeblock estates. It was all beautifully bleak and just as I remembered it. I was glad that everything around was being pummelled with black winter rain, painting the perfect picture for Dad, but when I glanced across at him I realised he probably wasn't taking much of it in. His eyes were staring hard and straight ahead, looking for risk through the rain. We passed the last groups of estate houses and bobbled down the gravel road and the building loomed into sight, a dark, rain-lashed shadow ahead. I told Dad to pull over at the entrance to the drive and he stopped and turned the engine off. He glanced around, looking for clues. I pointed towards the sign standing to our right. He wiped the condensation from the inside of his window and peered and read. He looked back to me and asked what this was all about, why had I brought him here? I told him: because Jon brought me here. Because this is where he will end up; it's the only place they could put him. Dad was already turning the car around in the tight lane as I spoke, turning it to face Duerdale Fell and the drive home. I couldn't read his face at all. I couldn't tell what he was thinking, if he was angry or not. We drove back to the house in silence and parted at the front door. I went straight up to my room and Dad went to his workroom.

It was late when he knocked at my door. A tentative tap that wouldn't wake me if I was sleeping. I was in bed but a world away from sleep and said to come in. Dad slipped past the door, crossed the room and sat at the foot of my bed. I sat up, turned my lamp on and blinked heavily, shutting out the glare. Dad said he was sorry if he'd woken me and I told him he hadn't, that I wasn't even tired. He rested his hands on his knees and started asking questions about Jon. About how he came to live with his grandparents, how long he'd lived on the fell and what I knew about his mum and dad. Did he have any other relatives? I answered as well as I could. I told him I didn't know how long Jon had lived here but I thought it was a few years. I told him his mum was dead and he never knew his dad. As for any other relations, he never mentioned anyone and I got the feeling that was because he didn't know of any.

Dad sat silent, considering the information I'd managed to give him.

'How would you feel about it?' he asked. 'Another person, here, all the time.'

I shrugged. 'Well, he's here a lot of the time anyway, isn't he?'

He nodded. 'He is, but this would be something else altogether. This isn't fish and chips, a video and a sleepover. This is responsibility.'

He meant it was responsibility for him.

'Mum wouldn't have even had to think about it.'

He didn't flinch, didn't move a millimetre. I lay awkwardly, half propping myself up, arms aching, waiting for his response. He carried on sitting with his hands on his knees, staring ahead. Eventually he stood up and turned my lamp off. 'I know,' he said. 'Get some sleep.'

Pamphlets, leaflets and forms

'I'll phone them,' he said the next morning. 'That Mr McGrath, I'll speak to him. See what he has to say.' I carried on eating my cornflakes. He looked across at me. 'But things like these, Luke, they're never simple. Don't get ahead of yourself. And don't say anything to Jon.'

He phoned Mr McGrath that afternoon. He explained why he was ringing, what he was thinking, and then waited for a list of reasons why it wasn't feasible. He waited to hear that there were waiting lists, regulations, procedures and processes. But Mr McGrath just told him to come in for a chat the next day. So after he dropped me off at school Dad drove to the red Social Services building in town and found Mr McGrath's small and cluttered office. They talked about Jon. They spoke about his situation. It was very sad, they said. Tragic. They shook their heads. Two men on the same side. Then Mr McGrath turned his attention to Dad. How did he know Jon? How long had Jon been coming to the house? Did Dad have any contact with Jon's grandparents? How did I feel about it all? How did he think Jon would feel about the idea? Did Dad realise that there would be police checks, interviews, references requested? There would be scrutiny. Dad was bombarded for the next twenty minutes. He left with a mountain of pamphlets, leaflets and forms. He was told to read them all and to think hard about how serious he was about all of this.

When I got back from school I didn't find him in his workroom as usual. He was sat at the table by the front window that looked out onto the falling fields and further down onto Duerdale. All the paperwork was scattered in front of him. The sun was already setting and the town's lights were beginning to come on. The long, straight bypass that cuts across the length of the valley was the first to light up and it always reminded me of a runway at night. The town followed. A cluster of lights springing on and lighting up the estates to the south of the town and the terraced streets nearer the centre. It looked like a golden spider web settling into the black of the valley, an ugly town turned pretty for the night. He glanced up when I walked in and he looked like he'd just got off a long-haul flight. I asked him if he was all right and he stood up slowly, stretched and twisted and said he was. He'd just been thinking, that was all, thinking all afternoon.

Dr Abdelbaki knew that Dad wasn't related to Jon. And so did all the nurses. Mr McGrath probably told them. But nobody seemed that concerned. They knew that Arthur and Edna Mansfield were two wards below, probably not long for this world; they knew the background and they were pleased someone was taking an interest. Mr McGrath and Ms Green had been visiting Jon regularly and I thought he would have little time for them. I thought that they were the sworn enemy, that he would stare ahead, refuse to make eye contact, fold his arms and bury his chin in his chest. But it wasn't like that at all. Maybe it's like Mum said, things are only rarely as bad as your imagination can make them. Now Jon was slap bang in the middle of his nightmare, now it was happening, maybe it just wasn't quite as nightmarish as he'd imagined.

He visited his grandparents on their ward during the days. He received the same confused stare from his gran that everyone received, and Jon admitted that she'd been like that for months now. But he sat with her every day. He changed the water in her glass and tidied her bedside table. When she said incomprehensible things about people he'd never heard of, people he wasn't sure had ever existed, he nodded as if it all made sense. When she was agitated and scared, shouting out, he tried to calm her. He told her she was safe. He held her hand.

Jon's granddad had calmed down since his kidnapping. He was resigned and tired. Remarkably he and

Jon never spoke about the day they were dragged from their home and brought to the hospital. And they never spoke about what might happen next. Jon said he would try but his granddad would get annoyed, wave him quiet and tell him not to be bothering trouble. And Jon said that he'd always been like that. Even when his mum died, when he was dumped on their doorstep, they just opened the door and let him in, made up a bed and carried on. Things were as they were and they muddled through. When Jon arrived from his ward to sit with his gran for a while Arthur would drag himself to the hospital garden and sit on a bench in the corner and look up to the sky or just stare ahead. I saw him out there a couple of times, and part of me wanted to go and sit with him. But I knew I never would; I couldn't think of one single thing to talk to him about. And I just didn't dare.

Dad had reached a decision and he seemed sure. He said we would give it a go. See what we could do – if that was all right with me. If it wasn't, it wouldn't go any further. We'd stop it now. He thought we should have a big chat, I could tell. He kept saying that this was a life-changing decision and he wanted to know my views. I told him we had no choice; it was just something we had to do. He got annoyed at that and said that it wasn't just something we had to do. We had to make a conscious decision whether or not to go ahead and it would affect me just as much as it would affect him. I should think about what it would actually mean on a day-to-day basis. So I shrugged. That annoyed him even more. I knew it would. Sometimes it's fun. But he knew what I thought. He was just annoyed that he wasn't getting his big discussion. He was annoyed that I wasn't saying that I knew it would be tough for him but it was the right thing to do. Well done, Dad. I just didn't feel like joining in and I really did think that we didn't have a choice. It was clear to me. He was right about one thing though. We had to speak to Jon. Neither of us knew what he thought about the whole thing.

It was getting late and Jon was tucked up in bed and it was only a few minutes until chucking-out time and Dad still hadn't said anything. Some visitors at other beds were already pulling coats on and checking pockets for keys. I kicked at Dad's leg underneath the bed. He glared at me. He cleared his throat and told Jon something that he already knew – that he would have to live somewhere else from now on. Jon nodded that he understood that to be the case. There was a pause before Dad asked how he would feel if the house he came to stay at was ours. Jon didn't look at either of us. Just said quietly that it would be brilliant. Dad said, 'Well, we'll see what we can do, eh? See what happens . . . It's out of my hands really so no promises.' There was silence. Jon rubbed a tear into his cheek. Dad exhaled and looked up at the ceiling fan. I looked across Jon's bed and saw the three of us reflected in the black window and started to laugh like a lunatic. I held my hand over my mouth and nose and tried to keep it down and hold it in but it bubbled up and sprayed out anyway. Dad looked annoyed and Jon looked shocked. I managed to calm myself and stifle the laughs and I apologised. I said it was just because I was nervous. And although that is true, I do laugh when I'm nervous, it was really the sight of the three of us, reflected back in the hospital window that set me off. We looked so gormless and mismatched and bloody useless. But we were having a go at least. You can't say we weren't doing that.

I didn't dare look at the reflection for the next few minutes in case it set me off again but it was nearly chucking-out time anyway. Dad told Jon that he would have to talk to his granddad to see what he had to say about it all and Jon nodded that he would and then we grabbed our coats to leave. We left the ward and joined the exodus of relatives and friends back to the car park. When we got out into the cold night air Dad stopped. He rammed his hands deep into his coat pockets, leant against a pillar and breathed heavily in and out for a few seconds before jogging across the car park to catch me up.

Chuck

The day I cracked Kieran Judd's head against a wall like it was an egg I threw up. I was lying on my bed after school, not even thinking about anything and then I was suddenly prickly hot. Colours flashed behind my eyes and my whole body went slack and I knew what was coming. I managed to make it to the bathroom on jelly legs just in time to kneel over the toilet and heave. The walls of my belly closed in and I was sick three times. Three full retches that tore my tummy muscles and filled the bowl. I flushed the smell away but waited by the toilet, making sure I'd emptied myself fully. When I'd decided it had all come out I washed my face, rinsed my mouth and cleaned my teeth. I went back to bed but I was cold now, trembling, and I wrapped the covers tight around me. Dad tapped on my door and asked if I was OK. I told him I was, that there was a bug going round, that was all. He padded away and it was only then that I thought about what had happened with Kieran Judd. And it shocked me who I'd been for those two minutes. I don't even like watching violence in films; I always turn away when things get particularly bad or gruesome. I always was the delicate artist. I couldn't be sorry though; I didn't think I'd done anything wrong. It was simple: it needed to be done and it had to be me who did it. I just hoped that I didn't have to do anything like it ever again. But I would do if I had to. I might read books and paint pictures but I'm not soft.

Hospital garden bench

The meeting between Gerald Redridge and Arthur Mansfield took place in the hospital garden on a cold but bright Wednesday afternoon. God knows how they managed a conversation. Here were two men, normally as silent as gateposts, sitting side by side on a wooden bench, having to address a subject that neither really wanted to address at all. I would've loved to have been there. Even just to count the words that passed between them. It couldn't have been more than seventeen surely?

I was stuck at school though and spent the afternoon staring out of dirty windows at empty playing fields and wondering what was happening two and a half miles away.

Mr McGrath had been visiting Jon's granddad regularly and had already made him aware that it was impossible for Jon to live at the farmhouse any more. The legal side of things, whether or not Arthur and Edna Mansfield were ever officially Jon's legal guardians, seemed to be a fact that nobody could trace, an issue that nobody was too certain about. But Mr McGrath said that, in a way, it didn't really matter any more anyway. Neither of them were able to provide adequate care for Jon, so it had become irrelevant. Mr McGrath had already told Arthur about the idea, the possibility, that Jon could live with us and Jon himself had hinted something similar. So Dad wasn't going in cold. Arthur Mansfield had been briefed. Dad was still nervous though and when he dropped me off at school he told me to wish him luck in telling a frail old man he'd come to take his grandson away.

The night before the meeting Dad asked Jon if there was anything his granddad particularly liked: was he partial to a particular brew of beer or brand of whisky? But that idea was quickly dismissed when Jon's face turned from its usual white to a death white. It turns out that Arthur wouldn't have drink in the house, had never had a drink in his life, and probably wouldn't want to start now. Dad managed to calm Jon down; he promised he wouldn't take any alcohol and it was agreed that it might be best to turn up empty-handed anyway.

I was impatient to know how the meeting had gone, but I had to wait until the end of school and endure the bus trip home and then the long walk down the lane to the house. I hurried inside and found Dad in the kitchen, nursing a coffee. He looked up, guilty, like I'd caught him skiving or something. He said that he'd tried to get on with some work when he'd got back from the hospital, but he hadn't been able to settle to anything, he couldn't stop his mind wandering. I bombarded him with questions but he waved me quiet and said if I gave him a second he would tell me what happened.

He made himself another coffee, I sat down, and he told me the conversation they'd had, sat on the wooden bench. Dad had done most of the talking and it went OK, he said. Sad, but OK. He told Arthur that they were neighbours and that Jon had been visiting us for a few months now. Arthur nodded. Dad said he was sorry, the situation they found themselves in was hard. It was horrible. He stopped talking as an old lady with two walking sticks approached. She passed slowly. Her tongue stuck out of the top left corner of her mouth. She was concentrating hard. Focused. They stared ahead until she passed. He'd grown fond of Jon, he said, and would like to help if he could. Arthur still didn't respond and they sat in silence; Arthur occasionally looked up to the sky and the slow-moving clouds. Dad turned to him and asked if he knew about the idea, the thinking, that Jon could maybe live with us. Arthur nodded that he did and then, finally, he spoke. He asked if that meant Jon would be staying on the fell. Dad replied that yes, if it went ahead, it did mean that, for the foreseeable future at least. Arthur considered this and said that was good, that it would be good to be able to think of him up on the fell, in the fields, walking the lanes and tracks. They sat quietly then, watching people in varying states of health walking, wheeling and wobbling the circuit of the hospital garden. 'And then I started blathering,' Dad said. He said that it was to fill the silence more than anything; he couldn't leave so soon, and they couldn't just sit there in silence all afternoon.

He said he told him about the horse and the forest and dragging the pieces there, the toys he made and the markets he visited. He told him about me and Jon, how we were good mates. How good we were for each other. The odd couple.

'And I told him about your mum. About how daft and beautiful she was. How much fun she got from being alive and knitting a scarf, or going on a trip to the seaside, something simple like that. I told him that her joy made me feel glad to be alive, made me enjoy everything more. And I told him what a good wife she was, and what a wonderful mum she was.' He stopped. 'I'm sorry I've been so useless since she died, Luke.'

I shook my head.

'I have been. What have I done? How have I helped you? Have I spoken to you about her? Checked how things are at the new school? Helped steer you through a difficult time? No, I've got pissed and built a bloody massive bloody wooden horse to shove in the corner of a forest.'

'It's bloody good though, Dad,' I said.

He looked across at me. He considered. He nodded slowly and said, 'It is good, at least there's that.'

Climb and slide

In the evenings, in the hour before we went to bed, we'd started playing snakes and ladders. It was an accident how it started really. The board had been amongst all the junk the Thornbers had left and we found it during our half-hearted clearing out. For some reason Dad hadn't chucked it away and it had been lying on top of a pile of stuff we had no idea what to do with in the corner of the kitchen. One night Dad picked the board up, waved it at me and asked if I fancied a game. I shrugged and said why not. There was a dice knocking around, but no counters so Dad used a ten-pence coin and I was a twenty. We played about ten games the first night; Dad started to keep score, and it became a ritual that took place at the kitchen table most nights.

It was deep winter now and the kitchen was the warmest room. And it was the one room where Dad had got round to doing some work. He'd painted the walls and ceiling and stripped the kitchen cabinets and painted those too. He'd sanded the floorboards and varnished them and now there were no sharp bits of wood or rusty nails waiting to tear at your feet. He'd even hung some new curtains he'd bought cheap at one of the markets where he ran a stall. And it looked good. It was almost cosy. Dad drank coffee, me tea, and we would play game after game.

I'm not sure why I enjoyed it so much but it was part

of the day I looked forward to. It occupied me. And I found it relaxing, probably because there's nothing you can do to influence the outcome so you just sit back and watch how things turn out. And the worst thing that can happen is you are a roll of the dice away from winning and you land on the biggest snake on the board and slide back to square number three. We were playing so many games that it didn't matter anyway. And some nights it would all go your way. Every throw of the dice would dance you directly to the foot of the ladders, sending you skipping over each snake's flickering tongue, shooting you to the top of the board. And then there were the nights when you couldn't get above the third row. So you'd sit back and watch yourself slip back down to the bottom. Over and over again. And in some ways that was almost as much fun as winning. I discovered that the acceptance of defeat is quite satisfying. We would play until Dad would think that enough was enough, and he would tell me one more game then bed. But as long as I was quick enough to start the next game as soon as we finished the last one, he would forget he'd said anything and we would play another five times before he would remember, grab the dice and fold the board away. At the end of each night he would add up the scores and pin the sheet to the back of the kitchen door. I was winning by 211 to 185, but that didn't matter. It was just satisfying to talk about nothing in particular, keep rolling the dice and watch the score grow ever bigger every night.

Mr and Mrs Theobalds

Jon was discharged. He ended up with Mr and Mrs Theobalds. A middle-aged couple who live in a semi on a boring street in Duerdale. He works at the bank in the middle of town and she's an administrator for Tunnel Cement. On Thursday nights they play badminton in a mixed league at the local sports centre. They aren't very good really, but they enjoy the social side of it and it helps keep them fit. They have two grown-up kids who've left home and moved away and who only make it back for Christmas and big birthdays. For the last twenty years they've offered short-term foster care to children whose lives are in limbo, whose lives have reached a crisis point. They provide shelter for a few days or weeks before a decision is reached and the child disappears. Sometimes it goes well, everyone gets on and the child remembers them fondly and grows up and sends them a card at Christmas and then photos of their own children. Other times it's trickier. Fifteen-year-old Julian Rodgers smashed every window in the house and pissed on their bed when they at were badminton one Thursday. They had to stay at a hotel that night. Even the Theobalds' legendary patience was tested to the limit on that occasion. But like Mr Theobalds said the next day when the glaziers were fitting the new glass and their scrubbed mattress was drying in the back garden and he'd had time to reflect: if what'd happened to Julian had happened to him, he said, he'd probably smash a load of windows and piss on a bed.

Red arrows

The day after the fight in the empty classroom Kieran Judd approached me in the main corridor, pulled me aside and told me that it wasn't finished. He seemed distracted and spoke calmly, like he was saying that maybe the weather could turn to rain. I asked what he meant but he just said that I would see and walked off. I tried to stay in busy places and made sure that I wasn't left alone. I braced myself. I jittered and jumped every time someone brushed past or a hand was rested on my shoulder. And for day after day nothing happened. So I persuaded myself to forget about it and I let my shoulders drop. We'd had a fight and I'd smashed his head open and that was all I needed to remember.

Now Jon was living in town it was easy for him to walk to school and we agreed to meet on his first day back outside the front gates. It had been three weeks since he'd been discharged from hospital and he was looking stronger and healthier than I'd seen him. Dad dropped me off as usual and I stood and watched the gaggle of burgundy blazers rush and dawdle and splinter and group, as clumsy as a herd of cattle, up the road towards me. Even this early there were arguments and shrieks, squeals and flirting, everything being set up for the day. I tried to ignore the hubbub; I was on the lookout for one lone head amongst it all, bobbing along, eyes to the floor, with a too-big bag slung over his shoulder. Gradually the pack thinned and now it was just down to the stragglers, racing up the road, not even glancing at me as they shot past, intent on beating the bell. I was about to give up and answer the bell myself when two sprinting figures slipped into focus and I saw Judd and Laycock charging towards me. They swept past like red arrows and just for good measure Judd gobbed in my ear. I was reaching into my pocket to find something to mop it out when he shouted back to me, 'When you find him, make sure you tell him it's your fault.' I shouted, 'Where?' but they were already gone and my question only banged into the closed doors of the school.

I rubbed at my wet ear with my sleeve and set off. The Theobalds' house was on Cowper Avenue which was a ten-minute walk or a five-minute run. I ran straight down the school road, right past a couple of scruffy tennis courts, across an old iron bridge over the River Hodder and onto waste ground where some falling-down garages stood. Cowper Avenue started just two roads behind here and I threw myself along these quiet morning streets as fast as I could. But I made it to the end of Cowper Avenue and had found nothing. I stopped and tried to think and wondered for a second if it had been a wind-up. The only place I could think where I might have missed him was the wasteland with the tumbledown garages so I ran back and started trying the doors of the garages, shouting his name. I peered through mucky windows into dark spaces full of crap and nothing but he was nowhere about. Unless they'd had time to drag him further away he was safe at school and I was late. I turned to walk back to school and heard the shout.

Under the iron bridge

The voice came from the direction of the bridge. I ran and stopped halfway along and listened again. I heard nothing but a roar in my head and the booming stomp of my heart. I went to the left-hand side, jumped up, clung on, and looked over and saw only the grey river shouldering its way underneath. Then I heard another shout. It came from behind, from the opposite side. I crossed the bridge in three steps, jumped up again and peered over and looked down onto the top of Jon's head.

He was stood on a thin ledge, with his back flat to the bridge, with about an inch to spare to the drop. He was staring down at the river. I asked him what the hell he was doing and his head tipped back and terrified eyes stared up at me and I could see from his face and the state of his clothes that they'd only left him on the ledge as an afterthought, after the beating. I told him to give me his hands and I'd help him climb back, but he turned carefully to his left and showed me that his hands were tied behind his back with his school tie. I climbed over onto the ledge and untied him and he managed to scuffle himself back onto the bridge but he didn't stop shaking for a good twenty minutes. The beating was a bad one and he had marks on his face and scrapes on his legs and broken blood vessels were probably already flowering into bruises underneath his skin. We slowly walked back to Cowper Avenue. After we'd been sat for a while and after the shaking stopped I told him the truth. I told him what happened that day in the empty classroom and what Judd had said to me that morning. I asked him what he wanted to do next and his answer was a definite nothing. He said maybe now I could see that this is what happens when you try and do something This is what you get for fighting back.

Ramshackle

Dad put the phone down and said 'Bollocks.' All the forms had been filled in. All the checks were being made. All the references written and signed and dated. He thought he just had the final interview to get through and that would be it. But there was another hurdle and it was the equivalent of the water jump on the last lap of the steeplechase. It was something neither of us had even thought about and it was something that for most people wouldn't be an issue. But for us it might be . . . They were coming to check the house. Dad went back to his file and pored over all the forms and pamphlets, and sure enough, there it was, in the WHAT TO EXPECT booklet.

26B INSPECTION OF PROSPECTIVE CARER'S ACCOMMODATION
A carer's home must be warm and furnished and decorated to a high standard. All rooms must be kept clean and hygiene must be seen as a priority by the prospective carer. The home and immediate environment must be free of hazards and anything that might expose a child to any risk of injury or harm.

I looked around at the state of the place. Suddenly the stains on the walls seemed darker. Nails poked out of uneven floors. The furniture looked ramshackle. There were gaps in the banister. There were loose and ancient plug sockets. Hazards leapt out like never before. Dad had tackled the kitchen, it was where we spent most of our time, but nothing else had been touched since we moved in. The leaflet set out in detail what was expected of a carer's home and as Dad read down the list his head-shaking grew more intense. He passed the list to me and I saw he was right to be worried. But at least they'd rung. At least we'd been given a warning. We had two days until the visit. And it wasn't like we lived like animals; we weren't unhygienic. It just seemed impossible to make this house look clean. The walls were too dark, there were too many old and badly decorated rooms. And even though we'd already made two trips to the local dump, clutter still congregated and clung in every corner. And maybe we had let things slip a little. Maybe we weren't quite as conscientious as we should have been. Perhaps our clothes weren't washed quite as often as they used to be and the washing-up wasn't done as regularly as it could be.

Dad walked from room to room. Kicked a piece of furniture. Stroked a patch of wall. He came back into the kitchen and told me he was going out and he would be about an hour. He banged out of the front door and I watched our battered old Volvo disappear down the fell track with smoke belching out from the exhaust. I thought about making a start on the house but didn't know where to begin. So I did half an hour of washing-up and put some dirty clothes in the machine. Just as it was kicking into mental spin Dad returned and shouted to the house for my help.

The boot was open and the car was filled with tin after large tin of bright white economy paint. We lugged them into the hallway and Dad put the kettle on. He sat me down, and told me the plan. For the next two days I had gastric flu. He would ring the school and explain why I wouldn't be attending. I asked why it had to be gastric flu but he waved me quiet. We would move all the old junk that we hadn't got rid of yet and dump it behind the outhouse and have a bonfire. Then we would paint every room white. We would, he said, just slap it on. We weren't to worry about neatness, about tidy edges and masking tape. We didn't have time. We were going for the bigger picture, creating an impression of cleanliness and space. If he got time he would try and look at the floors, sort out the plug sockets and other smaller jobs. It would be hard work, but hopefully, with the two of us working flat out, it could be done. After two hours of dragging heavy and dirty furniture from every corner of the house to the back of the outhouse I thought of Jon. Tucked away in his warm, clean bedroom. Rereading *Planets, Stars and the Universe* for the twentieth time. And I thought to myself, the lucky bastard.

Interiors need updating

It was knackering. But we got rid of all the junk and the house looked ten times better already. We kept some of the chairs, the kitchen table and the ragged and stained three-piece suite. I thought there was no way Dad would want anyone to see that but when he saw me dragging the settee towards the back door he shouted at me to stop, pulled it back to the lounge and said, 'Throws, Luke. Five quid each at the market. Cover a multitude of sins.'

I managed to bite my tongue and not ask why, if they were that cheap, and he saw them every other day, he hadn't bought them six pissing months ago. Almost everything else went on the pile though. We were ruthless and it only seemed a shame that we had missed November the 5th. The bonfire was the fun bit. We stood and watched years of battered and tatty Thornber history go up in flames. We toasted the old couple with cups of tea and watched as the flames crackled and spat and then burnt into smoke and drifted across the fell.

Then the real work started. There had been a change of plan and I was to start painting by myself. Dad was going to make a start with the floor sander he'd hired. I thought that was unfair, that he'd got the fun job. But then I saw how hard and slow it was, and how much floor space he had to cover, and I was pleased I was on painting duty. I slunk away and left him sweating and swearing and covered in dust.

I started in what would be Jon's bedroom and thought I was doing OK until Dad came into the room and laughed when he saw the progress I'd made. I thought I'd done a pretty good job but we needed to be quicker, he said, and we should only use the brushes on corners.

He poured half a tin of paint into a tray, grabbed one of the big rollers and rolled it over a section of the wall. He covered as much in thirty seconds as I'd done in my half an hour. After I'd been shown the trick I cracked on and finished Jon's room in a couple of hours. I finished upstairs at about nine that night.

We were too tired to play snakes and ladders; Dad just warmed up a pizza and we sat in the bare front room and ate off our laps. I said I was knackered. Dad said it was a break from dragging wood through a forest. I asked how the sculpture was going and when we could see it.

'Shortly,' he said. 'Nearly there.'

With my dad, that could mean tomorrow or next Christmas. You never could tell. My heart spun when I saw him bring in a whisky bottle and pour himself a measure, but he told me it was just a small drink, just to relax, that we had another busy day tomorrow. And I checked the bottle before we went to bed and it looked like just one or two had been poured.

The next day followed a similar pattern but Dad finished sanding the floors and started helping me with the painting. We had a brief break for lunch, ate more pizza in the evening and then carried on working. Dad even managed to varnish some of the floors downstairs and got started with some of the smaller jobs. He replaced the missing wood in the banister and had a go at making the plugs safer. I didn't know if they would pass any tests, but at least you didn't worry about pulling the socket out from the wall when you unplugged the kettle any more.

Dad had bought throws and got more light bulbs and light shades and a couple of lamps and some picture frames. It was almost midnight when all the painting had been finished and when he started screwing in the light bulbs and fitting light shades. I was collapsed on the settee, my eyes flickering, my legs jerking out in sleep spasms. I stretched myself awake and said it was pity we didn't have anything to go in the frames. Dad looked at me like I was simple and told me that paintings were one of the few things we had loads of. I managed to stay awake a few minutes longer but by the time he started to bang nails into walls I was gone and sleep was swallowing me. I dragged myself up to my brand new bedroom and climbed into bed without taking my paint-splattered clothes off. I fell asleep in a second, despite the banging, clattering and occasional swearing from downstairs.

White walls and red throws

The next morning my body ached and groaned at every tense and twitch. Joints were rusty hinges, muscles as heavy as pistons. Standing up hurt, sitting down hurt, even cleaning my teeth hurt and I grumbled as I pulled on my uniform. I'd moaned the day before about having to go to school when there was still stuff that needed doing to the house but Dad made the point that I could hardly be seen at home, skiving, by the Social Services Family Placement Team.

I walked down the stairs that morning into a new house. I'd been too tired the night before to see what we'd achieved in the previous forty-eight hours. And judging by the further progress made, Dad must have continued long after I went to bed. I found him asleep on the settee, hugging himself, mouth wide open and the warm smell of sleeping man fugging up the room. I didn't wake him; I wanted to enjoy our new home alone for a few minutes.

The sun threw itself through the windows and onto our work. The snowball-white walls contrasted with the crimson-red light shades and the matching throws on the settee and chairs. I couldn't help thinking that Dad had chosen well, that his eye for detail had been put to good use. My eyes were drawn to the floor, to the smooth brown surface. No longer grey and rough, no nails in sight. In each room hung a couple of my paintings. In the lounge were two paintings of the stones at the top of the fell. In the hallway he'd hung two paintings of a derelict barn. I'd painted them on different days. One was done on a crisp, clear day like today. The other was painted on an early-winter evening with a Lucozade-orange sky hovering above the dark, crumbling barn.

Dad had woken and padded his way into the hallway. Despite his moaning about how quickly the damp would come through, I could tell he was pleased with the place. Pleased with how it had turned out. And for the first time since we'd moved to Duerdale, for the first time in months, I was somewhere I didn't want to leave. I was sad to climb into the car and go to school and sit in scruffy classrooms in itchy trousers for hours. I was nervous throughout the day. I was worried that when I opened our front door at the end of the afternoon it would have turned back into the dirty old house it had been for the last thirty years.

But when the bus dropped me off at the end of our lane I could see lights burning in rooms that had never had light bulbs before. And when I got through the door I saw plants in pots in corners of the hallway. There was even a doormat inside the front door with a picture of a cat in a hammock and 'Home, Sweet Home' across the bottom. I thought that might be too much. He'd varnished doors and fixed dodgy handles. All the washing-up had been done and put away. The place was immaculate. I found him in the lounge, collapsed on the settee, messing up a throw. When he saw me walk in the room he said, 'Hello, Luke, guess what?' I lowered myself carefully into one of the chairs and said, 'What?'

'The bastards have just rung. They're not coming till next week now.' He laughed like a lunatic, shouted 'Jesus Christ!' at the ceiling and told me to put the kettle on.

Bring the camera

The horse was finished. Finally. Dad had been working on it whenever he got the chance. When all the pieces were in the clearing, he'd assembled it, repainted it, and made all the adjustments he always made. Slowly inching the piece over the finish line, working until he was happy with every view from every angle. It was a Saturday morning when we all went to see it in its new home. This time when Dad pushed through the green iron gate and started weaving between the trees, he didn't need a map or notes. He knew the route well; he could probably do it on a moonless night. And maybe me and Jon could have found the way too. There were clues now every few yards – footprints and broken twigs on the floor. Lines torn through the green mossy mounds where Dad had given up carrying a limb and decided he would have to drag it instead. A footpath had started to emerge between the trees.

We moved faster than last time and nobody needed to stop and rest. Dad checked a few times to see that we were keeping up OK, and we were, and it felt like we made it to the clearing in about half the time it took on the previous visit.

Me and Jon chatted as we walked, saying we were sure we recognised the strange-shaped tree that must have been shocked into position by lightning, or we didn't remember that stream running away to the left. But as we got closer to the clearing, we fell quiet and I was aware of our feet cracking twigs and our legs swish-ing through ferns, the pulling of a zip and the clearing of a throat. Every noise amplified in the silence.

It was a frosty morning and Dad must have been pleased when he pulled back his curtains to see white on the ground and the winter sun filtering through. We were the first people out and about and even the grim streets of Duerdale sparkled brightly as we drove through the silent early-morning town. In the forest our feet crunched and broke into the crispy ground and our breath blew cold smoke into the leaves as we pushed our way through the trees. Just as we were about to arrive Dad stopped and made us change direction. He walked us round to the right and up a steep slope so when we stopped and turned we were walking downhill towards the carving. He said it looked better approaching from this angle. The trees were clustered tightly here and as we trod forward, carefully stepping over roots, I got my first glimpse: a patch of white, leaping through the branches. Just for a second. And then gone. A few seconds later Jon got his first sighting and he said loudly, 'There! I saw it . . . just then . . .' But it disappeared as quickly for him as it had done for me. For a minute or two we were tricked and teased by further glimpses. A glance of a flank. A snapshot of a leg. Then Dad pushed past the final row of trees and stood to one side and we stepped out right behind him.

We walked out to see the horse from the side. The first time we saw him in Brungerley Forest he was a silhouette. His front legs kicking high. White against green. It was early enough for patches of mist to be lingering on the floor of the clearing and Dad's horse sparkled hard with frost. It looked better than any painting in any gallery I'd seen.

Dad had brought his old camera and took lots of pictures. Capturing it, he said, before it got weather-torn and tired. And then he made me and Jon stand in frame and took photos of us patting and stroking the horse. And then one of us just stood by it, looking back at him with stupid grins on our faces.

Portakabin calm

The day of Dad's big interview with Social Services we didn't go to school. We went to Jon's Portakabin. I didn't even know it existed. Neither of us planned it, but when we met outside school it felt impossible to walk though the gates and across the yard and into registration. We didn't want to get called sheepshaggers and sit in lessons with annoyed teachers and stupid kids all day. So we legged it. We ended up at the rec, sitting on the swings, surrounded by greasy fast-food paper stuck in the fences, shivering in the wind. The clouds sat on top of each other at the foot of the valley, rain was inevitable, and we had nowhere to go.

They'd set the date for the interview the day after they came to inspect the house. That had gone fine; lots of nodding. They'd seemed more interested in the view of Duerdale and the toys in his workroom, Dad said. Dad had been told that no individual step of the process carried more weight, that the final decision would be made taking all aspects of his application into consideration. But he didn't believe them. He said this was the big test. But he was ready. He'd done his research. He'd read all the booklets and he'd been on the internet. He'd been on the forums and he'd emailed people who'd been through the same process. He knew what questions to expect and he'd prepared answers. He'd even taken his grey Marks-and-Sparks suit out of the cupboard and hung it on the washing line to air. He meant business.

Dad's interview wasn't until four in the afternoon so

we had six hours to wait. Six hours of leisure time taunting us, on a winter's day in Duerdale. We should have gone to school. I swung limply on my swing. Jon didn't bother to move at all. He sat still, feet on the ground, hands holding the chains, staring across the rec. After a few minutes of cold silence he stood up grabbed his bag and told me to follow him and we went to his Portakabin.

It was hidden by low-hanging trees and years of untamed undergrowth and nestled on the lip of one of Tunnel Cement's abandoned quarries. You could see the quarries from up on our fell. They spread out to the left of Duerdale, taking up almost as much space as the town itself. On the edge of the quarries are the two tall chimneys that tower over the town. The chimneys pump out smoke constantly. Two giant, eternal cigarettes. If the wind is blowing in a certain direction, you wake in the morning to find that cars and windows in town are covered with a thin layer of white powder, like the police have been and dusted for fingerprints in the night.

Jon's Portakabin was long forgotten and unloved until he got his hands on it. He told me there was a key still in the door when he found it, and he left it there the first couple of times he visited. But when he was sure he was the only person who used the place, he pocketed it.

It took about ten minutes to walk to the site from the rec, to the edge of town and then we cross-countried through a few fields. As we drew close I could see the high perimeter fence, topped off with a rusting loop of barbed wire. It looked impenetrable. 'Watch this,' Jon said, and I looked at his slight frame and back at the tall fence and the rusting wire and was prepared to be amazed. It wasn't that amazing. He walked up to the fence, found his spot and pushed. He ended up on the other side in a second, grinning back at me. I got close and I could see the tiny tears where the fence had been cut. I was about to push my way through when I noticed a rusty yellow sign on a tree behind Jon. Big black letters informed that GUARD DOGS PATROL. Jon followed my eyes to the sign and said that in two years he'd never seen or heard a dog. I squeezed through the fence, quickly inspected the tear to my trousers and the scratch to my leg, and followed a fast-disappearing Jon through the trees.

I stayed close to Jon as he pushed and pulled himself through bushes and bramble. We scrambled through one last thicket and were there, facing the squat, grey, ugly cabin. Jon fished for the key in his pocket and pushed it into the lock. He turned the key and at the same time gently lifted the door upwards. It swung open smoothly and I followed him inside.

It was brilliant. He had bookshelves, a table and two chairs. A rug. Spotless and tidy. No clutter anywhere. He saw my expression and grinned. 'Some of this stuff was here already but I've added to it. I put the shelves up. The table and chairs were left by the workmen.'

I sat down and said, 'It's amazing.'

And Jon nodded. Not boasting, just agreeing.

'I used to come here all the time,' he said, 'before I started coming to yours.'

I went across to the bookshelves and pulled out *The RSPB Book of Birds*. It had the Dewey number still on the spine but when I opened it I saw the title page had been ripped out and WITHDRAWN had been stamped across the contents page.

'They sell them for almost nothing when they get a bit scruffy,' Jon said. 'They aren't allowed to keep them no matter how popular they are.'

I put the book back on the shelf and wandered around, getting a feel for the place, enjoying being in this secret world. Then I sat back down and we both stretched our legs out, like old men in front of a fire.

'This is brilliant,' I said.

The clouds that had been at the foot of the valley when we set off had caught us up and the sky turned black and the inside of the cabin darkened. There was a loud crack of thunder that echoed like a bomb in the surrounding quarries. The rain hit the Portakabin a few seconds later, drumming hard and fast onto the roof and streaming down the windows in rivulets. It didn't matter. We could wait there until it passed. It felt like we could wait there for ever. We sat in safe, dry silence and let the storm explode all around us.

Silent and grey

They don't tell you straight away. They write up a report and then it goes to a panel. Like Dad said, safety in numbers. He said the interview went as well as could be expected but that we should all wait and see and nobody should get their hopes up. I was disappointed,

Jon even more so, although he tried not to show it and he battled on as valiantly as usual. I think we both thought that it would be a sealed deal. That Dad would return with a takeaway from town and we would celebrate. But more waiting was needed and we were learning to add patience onto patience.

And of course Dad had to attend the interview with the police. We hadn't spoken about it since the night driving back from the hospital and I was worried it might send him grabbing for the whisky again. Leave him brooding in dark rooms. But there hadn't been any of that yet. There was no suit this time and I think he purposefully chose his scruffiest clothes before dropping me off at school and driving back to our old town and the police station.

I didn't know what I would come home to that day and I was irritated by everyone and everything at school. The stupid kids seemed even stupider than usual and the sarky teachers even more snide. I snapped and snarled my way through the day and didn't make friends with anyone. Lesson after lesson dragged by and it all seemed pointless and a waste of everyone's time. The tension finally poured away when I got home to find him in his workroom, working away, as if nothing upsetting had been discussed that day.

He told me to come in when I poked my head around the door and we sat down by his workbench and he told me what'd happened. The police asked questions about Mum, her medication and her state of mind at the time of the crash. Dad said that he answered the questions as honestly as possible and it was all over in a few minutes. But after he'd answered the last question and before they ushered him out of the interview room he said that he made sure he told them that it wasn't suicide. He told them that he knew his wife and on April the 11th at 4.27 p.m. it was not her intention to kill herself. He told them that it was a road accident and nothing else. I asked if he thought they believed him and he said he didn't know, he couldn't tell, but it didn't really matter what they thought. They just presented the information to the coroner who looked at all the facts and ruled on the cause of death. We had to wait; the inquiry and the ruling would be held two weeks on Thursday and we would find out then whether it would be ruled as suicide, accident or left as an open verdict.

'Just prepare yourself, that's all,' he said. 'Prepare yourself for whatever they might decide.'

That night, over snakes and ladders, I asked if he would write me a letter to get me out of school on the Thursday and he nodded that he would. We wouldn't be going to the inquest though, he said. We had a job somewhere else.

Idiot wind

It was half-term and we were in limbo. Vague time. Annoying days when even getting up seemed a waste of time, cleaning your teeth too much of an effort and doing just about anything else felt impossible. I was waiting; we were waiting for decisions to be made. Whether my mum drove her car into the front of a lorry on purpose or not was going to be decided by a group of people I'd never meet in a room I would never see. Dad's suitability to look after Jon was also being considered and although we knew Mr McGrath was involved, it still felt like we were waiting for a verdict from way up on high. All things out of our control.

All week I'd felt stuffy somehow. All my clothes felt too tight and I was hot and scratchy. It was like someone had rubbed dust into my eyes and pinned a duvet to my back and I shuffled round the house under the extra weight like an irritable old man. I tried not to be grumpy with Dad and Jon but I wasn't doing too good a job of it. And of course they had their own reasons to be grumpy and tense themselves. But I wasn't seeing too much of Jon anyway. He was way across the other side of town at the Theobalds' and spent most of his free time visiting his grandparents. They'd both been moved to Greenside Home for the Elderly. Jon said that one day he went to visit and couldn't find his granddad and the place was almost empty. He nearly fell over when a carer said it was always like this on a Tuesday morning: Tuesday was market day and a minibus turned up and took all those willing and able down to Duerdale market for an hour. Jon couldn't believe that his granddad had got on the bus and was currently browsing cheese and meat stalls. He said he was sure his granddad hadn't been into town for more than five years.

So it was mainly me and Dad and our irritation and anxiety. One afternoon he must have got fed up with my fixed face of misery and he told me to run to the other side of the fell or something. And although I don't think he actually meant it, I did run to the other side of the fell. And then down to the bottom. And then I got lost.

I'm not supposed to like sport. I'm a painter, an artist, and the two shouldn't really mix. And I don't like it much really; I can't stand games like football where someone on your own team shouts at you if you don't tackle hard enough. Or they get moody if you don't score when it's an easy chance. I'm exactly the kind of person who won't tackle hard enough or score when it's an easy chance. Running though is different. Unlike my dad I can't claim to be any good; I'm as bad at it as I am at every other sport, but I didn't mind the two times a year when we didn't play football and got sent on a cross-country run. Everyone else hated it, grumbled and moaned and pleaded with Mr Chisholm. I didn't care. At least nobody was going to kick me or shout at me.

I saw that it was pouring but I wasn't too bothered. I thought that might help with the stuffiness, it might help wash it away. I hunted down my sports kit and found it in the corner of my school bag. It hadn't been washed since the last time we'd had games and the green top and black shorts were melded together with dry mud that turned to dust when I tore them apart. I pulled them on anyway. They felt itchy and damp but it didn't matter. I would be as wet as a river in seconds anyway. I know the value in warming up and stretching, we get told every week at school, but I thought that running up and down the fell would warm me up well enough. And I was losing my spark of enthusiasm for the idea, so I did about three and a half star jumps, pushed open the back door and ran head first into the cold rain.

After about five minutes I nearly turned around and ran straight back. The wind was walloping sheets of rain into my face and I could hardly open my eyes to see. It was an icy-cold wind and it whipped blasts at my thighs and face. My face was numb and I couldn't feel the snot that flooded from my nose and over my lips. My hands were too cold to pull into fists and they were red raw and useless and struggled to open gates. The first part of the climb was too steep to run up properly and for the most part I scrambled up the fell, my hands touching the ground almost as much as my feet – a mountain goat without the sure-footedness. Finally I was on top of the fell and the ground flattened out. I passed the cairn, picked up speed and was actually running for the first time. I almost started to enjoy myself. The wind came in gusts from different directions, sometimes pushing me too fast ahead, my legs windmilling to keep up, sometimes a blast from the side and I wouldn't be running along the track any more but jumping through the heather and bracken, trying not to twist an ankle, trying to get back on course. I got a stitch just below my left ribcage. Sharp and hard, stabbing, like a needle was stuck inside. I didn't stop though. I ran at the pain. Head down, legs pumping. It was impossible to get any wetter or dirtier and I was heaving breaths in through my mouth, trying to get as much air as possible into my raw lungs. Snot was running down my face now as fast as I could wipe it away and I must have looked a mess. I wasn't feeling stuffy any more though. Sick, aching, numb and shattered, but not stuffy. And I discovered something that helped me focus, helped me keep going when I thought I might have to stop. I pictured a black rectangle with a red circle in the centre. And what I did was to concentrate on the red circle and poured all the pain and tiredness and breathlessness into it. Everything thrown at me: the wind, the rain, the almost vertical climbs, the loose rocks and the twisted ankles all went into the red circle. And I kept going. In half an hour I was at the far end of the fell, further than I'd ever been, and looking down onto towns and villages that I could only guess the names of. I allowed myself to stop and tried to grab some deep breaths of air from the wind. Even that wasn't easy. The wind dangled fresh air in front of my nose for a second before another gust stole it away, leaving me gasping in a vacuum. I rested my hands on my knees, tried to blow my nose clear and tried to recover. If I'd been feeling less frustrated and fed up I would have turned round and started making my way back home; darkness was edging itself into the corners of sky. But after a five-minute rest, I looked down at the sharp descent, let the muscles in my legs loosen, and legged it down the far side of the fell. I was enjoying the struggle.

Iron and fire

I discovered that it falls very dark very quickly on a fell in winter. By the time I got to the bottom of the other side it was dusk. Trees in the field ahead looked smudged and inky. Five minutes later everything was black. I didn't want to risk making the climb back up the fell in the dark so I would have to try and find a way around. I had vague memories of Jon talking about this side of the fell and I thought if I headed left I would eventually come to a small road that would lead me back to the main road and finally our house. It would take for ever, but it would be safer. I never did find a road though. After twenty minutes of running and falling through black fields I gave up. I considered my situation. I was on the wrong side of the fell, in the pitch black, in the rain, in my shorts. I started to shiver. I turned full circle on the spot and saw my only option. Twinkling lights three fields away. I hoped it was a farmhouse. I hoped they had a phone. I headed for the lights as quickly as I could on my cold and wobbly legs.

Normally I would hesitate at knocking on a stranger's door and asking for favours but I was in no position to be to embarrassed or shy. I banged my frozen fist against the door as hard as the pain would let me. My teeth started to chatter. A white-haired man pulled the door open wide and stood tall and solid in front of me, unfazed by the wind that ruffled his beard and shot past us both and into his house. I explained, as best I could through the shivering, that I was lost and asked if I could use his phone. He stood aside and let me in. He didn't seem surprised that a bedraggled boy in his dirty and wet school sports kit had just knocked on his door in the middle of nowhere half an hour after dusk. He told me to sit by the fire first, to get warmed up, and went to get me a towel. I sat on the edge of a dark leathery chair with a towel wrapped round my shoulders and held my hands out towards the orange and red coals. When my mouth calmed down enough for me to speak I told the white-haired man that my name was Luke Redridge, that I lived over the other side of Bowland Fell. He said, 'Pleased to meet you, Luke Redridge', and carried on reading his newspaper. When he could see I'd warmed up enough he took me through to his phone and I attempted to dial. It was an ancient phone. You had to put your finger in a little hole above the number and pull the dial as far as it would go to the right. Then you had to wait for the dial to spin back to where it started from before you could start with the next number. It took about twenty minutes to get to the end of our number. Finally it started ringing and thank God Dad was home. I asked if he could pick me up and he asked where I was. I put my hand over the receiver and asked the man where we were. He took the phone from me and gave Dad directions. Two cups of tea later I heard the Volvo pull up outside. I took a last swig and thanked the man for everything. He told me any time and didn't get up. I found my way back out of the house, walked out to the car and climbed in. As I pulled my seatbelt over, Dad asked if I felt better now. I nodded and said I definitely did. I told him I felt pretty good. He asked if I'd learnt anything and I said I had. If you have freezing-cold fingers, so cold you can't feel them any more, don't shove them in front of a burning-hot fire. It feels like your bones have turned to iron and are trying to tear their way out from underneath your skin.

It was the Thursday of the hearing and bloody early when Dad dragged me out of bed. He'd told me what job we had to do and I wouldn't say I was looking forward to it exactly but I was pleased it was finally being done. We were off to the coast with Mum's ashes and we were going out in a boat to scatter them at sea. Dad said it was important that we said goodbye to her in our own way, on our own terms, not in a courtroom with a bunch of strangers.

We picked Jon up in the middle of town. It might seem a strange trip to take him on but it was agreed that he must come when I told him what we had planned and he said that he'd never seen the sea before. I thought about some of the facts he'd told me over the last few months – that the Pacific Ocean occupies a third of the world's surface and covers more space than all the land put together. He told me that if you dropped Mount Everest into the Marianas Trench (the deepest part of the sea) its tip would still be covered by a mile of water. I thought about how awed he was by the idea of the sea and I hoped he wasn't going to be disappointed with a few square miles of the grey Irish Sea on an unremarkable winter's day.

Dad had spoken to people at various markets and made a few calls and eventually found a retired fisherman called Norman Hindle. Norman lived in Oakholme, a small coast town about an hour to the north and west of us. He said he would be happy to take us out a mile or two in his boat. When Dad explained the purpose of our trip Norman refused to take any payment so Dad asked around and found out he had young grandkids and loaded the boot with wooden toys.

Dad was in a strange mood on the journey. When we got out of the town and the rush-hour traffic disappeared he asked if we wanted some music for the drive. He turned the radio on before either of us answered him. I couldn't remember the last time we'd had music in the car. His shoulders were relaxed and his arms hung loosely from the steering wheel and he tapped along when a familiar song played. I thought I'd seen it all when he glanced over his right shoulder, dropped the Volvo down a gear and flew past two trucks and one car on the dual carriageway.

We arrived at Oakholme just after ten o'clock and followed the directions Norman had given. We pulled into a parking space overlooking the small harbour. As we came to a stop we could see a yellow boat, moored to the harbour wall. A grey-haired man was bustling around on the deck. We all clambered out of the car and as our doors slammed shut the grey-haired man looked up and waved a greeting to us. We all waved back at Norman.

The urn had been sat next to Dad on the front seat for the journey. It was a cheap-looking wooden box, made from balsa wood, the type of wood my dad sneered at and could hardly bring himself to touch. I had no idea how we'd ended up with it. Was Dad given a catalogue to choose from? Was there a choice of colours and materials? I never remember it being discussed. Dad carried the urn carefully in a green shoulder bag, his right hand holding it against his side like he was carrying a bomb. It was a strange walk down to the boat. Dad with Mum's ashes held against his side, me and Jon behind and only the sound of the sea gently wallowing into the harbour wall and the odd screech from a local gull.

Norman was brilliant. He acted like he did this kind of trip every day, like it was nothing unusual and there was nothing awkward about the whole thing. He welcomed us on board, gave us a quick safety chat and handed out life jackets. He told us how far out we would sail, in what direction and how long it would take. When we stopped he would ask if we were happy with the spot. He told us the conditions were favourable. The sea was, and should remain, calm. He said he understood that it was a difficult trip for us and he was pleased to be able to help in any way he could. He made a few last-minute checks and we were ready to go.

We sailed out from the coast for about twenty minutes. Me, Dad and Jon wandered around the boat, stared back at the coast and further out across the water. We looked down at the cold grey sea and watched the gulls above, shadowing our progress, expecting easy pickings. I wondered what was happening in a courtroom miles away. When Norman was happy we'd gone far enough he killed the engine and asked, 'Any good?' Dad looked to the empty horizon and back to the coast, towards Oakholme and the wooded hills and the little white houses that stood in line along the harbour and said, 'Yes, I think so. Luke?' I agreed that it seemed as good a spot as any. Norman told us that objects in the Irish Sea had been carried by tides as far north as Greenland and south to the tip of South Africa and that seemed to settle it.

Dad took the urn out of his bag and pulled the lid off. He kissed the box once on its side, held it out over the edge of the boat and gently poured some of the dust into the sea. He stood still for a few seconds, watching, and then passed the box to me. I copied him, kissed the box, and tipped until it was empty. It needed a hard shake at the end, just to get the last few flecks out from the corners. For a few seconds the ash in the water clung together like bubbles in a bubble bath then a wave broke it into two different groups and already now they were slowly drifting in different directions. Norman had retreated and was stood by the cabin of the boat. Jon was standing behind us, and me and Dad were leaning over the edge, watching the sea and ash sway below us.

And then it happened. It came out of the silence and calm as definitely as an aeroplane crossing an empty sky. The first thing I noticed was a shift in Norman's posture. His body tensed and he straightened his back. He was suddenly alert, nose in the air, like a dog catching a scent on the wind. The noise followed almost immediately. It was an immense, deep, terrifying roar. Like an army charging. The noise rushed in on us and I was suddenly aware of one half of the boat being higher than the other and then the other half rising quickly to catch up. In a second we were high and flat, on top of a huge wave, heads in the sky, above all the other water in the sea. For that second it felt like we were on top of a mountain with our heads touching pure air. Everything in the world seemed to hang in the balance. We fell as quickly as we had risen and crashed back to normal sea level. Dropping like a car off a cliff. The little boat rocked hard as we landed. It pitched left then right and only gradually calmed itself, eventually settling. We all stood with bodies braced and watched the wave roll away, further out into the sea.

The sound of silence

Nobody spoke. We stared at each other with hearts pumping blood fast through veins. All senses turned to ten. Each of us alert. Each of us massively alive. Norman gathered himself and took charge. He checked the boat. He asked if everyone was OK. We all nodded that we were. I think he was the most shocked out of all of us. He started the engine and turned us round to face Oakholme. He was keen to get us back to land. Jon asked him if that had been a Draupner-type wave. Norman said no, if it had been a Draupner-type wave we would all be at the bottom of the sea now. Still, he said, it was bloody big for the Irish Sea. Bloody big. As he sailed us back to shore, every few seconds he shook his head vigorously, shaking himself back to sense. All I could think about was how powerful the wave was that had pushed us up into the sky. And how helpless we were when it was happening. Part of me wanted me to rush back to land and cling to it and never let go. Part of me wanted to get straight back out to sea and sit and wait for ever for another wave like that.

It was only when Dad took Norman to the boot of our car and gave him the collection of wooden toys that conversation finally sparked into life again. Norman told Dad that he shouldn't have, that it was too much, and Dad replied that he wanted to, and it wasn't. And you could tell Norman was delighted. He held the toys up to the light, and opened and closed doors and spun wheels and said his grandkids would love them. Norman got ready to go then and we all said thank you and shook his hand and said our goodbyes. As he left he told Dad that if he ever wanted to go out again, to the same spot, or just for a sail, to give him another ring and to keep in touch. Dad said he would and part of me even believed him this time. It seemed like just the kind of thing Dad would enjoy – being on a small boat under an empty sky, miles from anywhere. And I could tell he liked Norman. He always liked people who made their point quickly and knew when to shut up.

We ate our sandwiches and crisps on a bench on the harbour and then Dad collected our rubbish and said we should be getting back. That news would no doubt be waiting. And it was. Just as we were settling ourselves into the car and readying ourselves for the return trip the phone in our freshly painted hallway was ringing out, startling an empty house. Half a minute later the red light started flashing, telling us we had a message. But we were still an hour and a half away from finding out that it was Mr McGrath at Duerdale Social Services. He was pleased to let us know that Mr Redridge had been approved as Jon Mansfield's foster carer. Could he call when he got chance to arrange to sign the papers?

Local artist, Gerald Redridge

Of course people found the horse. And they loved it. And as much as Dad said its origins would remain a secret, of course they didn't. It may have been a remote part of the forest, but people will notice a man dragging lumps of carved wood along. Particularly if it's happening regularly and the man is sweating and swearing and falling over and occasionally kicking a tree in frustration. There was even the dreaded article in the local paper although Dad drew the line at having his photo taken with the horse. The photographer kept saying, 'Come on, Mr Redridge, it's local interest, people will want to put a name to a face.' And Dad said, 'Exactly', and hid behind a tree. The photos looked brilliant though, they really did. And Dad didn't throw away that edition of the *Duerdale Advertiser* with the rest. He kept it hidden underneath some plans in his workroom.

And the council didn't mind. They just sent someone to check it was safe, that it wouldn't blow over in the wind. They were quoted in the article as saying that they would have preferred it if Mr Redridge had approached them before going ahead, but they couldn't argue with the magnificent end product of all his work. The Traditional Toy Makers Association even got in on the act with a quote about the consistent quality of the work produced by their long-standing member, Gerald Redridge. And they didn't mention the eleven years of unpaid subscription he owed them. Word got out and people went on special trips to find the carving. I was in a shop in town and I overheard a conversation: 'Have you been yet? Did you see it? No? I think it's in the north-west corner, I'll try and draw you a map, see if I can remember . . .'

But out of everyone in Duerdale who loved the carving, I'm sure it was me and Jon who loved it the most. I'll probably never really know what it means to Jon because I'll never ask. And I'm not sure I really know exactly what it means to me. All I know is that my dad could have drunk himself dead. He could've joined Mum and Brian Stuart. And I know he thought about it. I could see the weight that hovered above him during those months. But instead he built a massive wooden horse and dragged it piece by piece to the clearing. And now it stands deep in a hidden corner of Brungerley Forest. Created and constructed by the sweat and genius of Duerdale's local artist, my dad, Gerald Redridge. Sometimes we don't go and see it for weeks on end but it doesn't matter. We know it's not too far away. Wild-eyed and feet kicking high. Defiant.

Open

They found out that they didn't know. Or that they didn't know enough. Or something like that. They decided that Mum's death wasn't definitely an accident and it wasn't definitely suicide. But it might have been either. Or a bit of both. Maybe.

It didn't matter that the two people who knew her best in the world were convinced that it wasn't suicide. That was just hearsay and hunches. And that doesn't count. What counts are length and direction of tyre marks, road conditions at time of crash, toxicology reports, vehicle reports and angle of impact. And all of these things, in the case of Megan Redridge and her red Vauxhall Corsa and the collision with Brian Stuart and his enormous lorry on Crofts Bank Road on April the 11th at 4.27 p.m. didn't add up to anything conclusive. They just added up to two dead people and no explanation that could be written down. And when I heard I thought . . . OK . . . I see . . . right . . .

And I thought that everything would be fine because I knew that they were wrong and I'd already decided that it didn't matter what was said at the inquest. So I wasn't prepared for the anger that came later on that day when I was folding clothes away in my bedroom. It was a shock to me when it tore and spat into my blood and made me want to smash things until they were so small there would be no satisfaction in smashing them even smaller. This anger has dogged me since: it jumps out of cupboards and lurks behind trees and pounces at will. And every time I think I've managed to shake it off and balance everything cleanly and neatly and squarely in my head it floors me again and I have to stop whatever I am doing and take myself away to empty rooms and let it rampage its way around my head like a hurricane in a house. It leaves me frustrated and tearful and exhausted and still angry. I had no idea that a room full of strangers saying that they didn't know would fill me with so much fury.

I remember Dad telling me to think carefully, to consider how life would change with someone else around all the time. And I'd shrugged and ignored him and thought he was just thinking of excuses. But I had underestimated just how different everything would be. And sometimes, I did just want to scream to be left alone, to not have to think about someone else all the time. Sometimes it felt like me and Jon were each other's shadows, tripping over each other's heels, breathing each other's air. We got driven to school together, we spent lunch together, we got the bus back together and we ate together in the evening. Our bedrooms were next door to each other and we knew when the other one cleaned his teeth, went to the toilet and went to bed. And sometimes, I just wanted to disappear, to erase myself from it all and not always have to worry how someone else was feeling. It wasn't Jon's fault; it was nothing he said or did; he didn't change at all. But I saw it as my responsibility that he felt as settled as possible. And it was my responsibility because I had pushed for this to happen. But when I had to, I grabbed my painting stuff and headed for the hills or wherever. Jon seemed to understand that I wanted to be left alone and he never followed, he'd go to Greenside or to the Library or just read in his room. Sometimes I didn't paint at all but just sat for a couple of hours in Jon's Portakabin and read one of his dusty old books.

Of course it delighted the retards at school that we were living together and we were both asked where our boyfriend was all the time. Jon got through it with his usual head-down, oblivious-to-everything policy. I managed to ignore it most of the time too but occasionally snapped. It amazed me that even in a town as crap as Duerdale there were still strict divisions and cliques. And because me and Jon were from up on the fell, because we saw fields from our house and had to get a bus to school, we were the stupid, inbred yokels. I wanted to yell at everyone that the whole place was a shithole and as far as I was concerned they were all a bunch of inbred straw-munchers. I never snapped with Kieran Judd though. I'd learnt my lesson. And although nothing else had happened for a while I didn't know if it was an uneasy truce or if he was just biding his time. I tried not to aggravate him; just when things had settled down as much as they were likely to, I didn't want to be the one to start any more storms.

But then Jon's grandma died. It was horrible to see how the grief stamped all over him and tore him up. I think that Dad hoped I might swing into action and help pick up the pieces but the only thing I'd learnt was that there were no magic words, nothing really to be done, and like father like son I didn't say much to Jon at all. Dad patted him on the back when he got chance and I gave him a painting of Neptune I'd done for him, painted in the brightest blue paint I could find and framed in a silver frame. We all went to the funeral and I was as nervous as hell. I was worried that I might be sick, that I wouldn't be able to cope, but it was completely different to Mum's. The church was almost empty and nobody carried the gormless shocked expression that seemed to be the only look going at Mum's funeral. There were several old women there who treated it as a chance for a catch-up and Jon didn't even know who they were. The only people in the church who showed any signs of grief were Jon and Arthur and I was certain that occasionally, deep in Arthur's expression, I noticed a tiny flicker of relief that it was over now. Jon sat in the front pew next to his granddad, and me and Dad sat three rows back. The vicar clearly had no idea who had died and hadn't got much out of Arthur so it was a brief affair with all the usual stuff about full lives lived and resting in peace and all that crap. The vicar's voice was fake solemn and quiet and a rainstorm was hammering away outside so some of his words disappeared completely but nobody leant forward in an effort to hear. When it was over Dad asked Arthur if he wanted to come up to the house for something to eat but he shook his head. He looked exhausted and spent and said he just wanted to go back to Greenside. He looked like he was about ready to jump head first into a coffin himself and I hoped he could stick around a bit longer for Jon's sake. Jon was quieter for a few days, for a few weeks, but gradually he started getting back to his old self. We did occasionally speak about death and what might happen afterwards and all that kind of stuff and it was a shock to me to learn that for someone obsessed with fact and science he had an unshakeable belief in God and the afterlife. I wasn't going to start banging on about Darwin and evolution, the planet being billions of years old, dinosaurs, and how faith is just a security blanket for people too scared to look at life and see it exactly for what it is. I stayed quiet. He knew what I thought anyway.

Goodbye

Me and Jon spoke about the wave the whole time though. Maybe we were checking with each other that it really did happen. Dad was less silent these days, but it was something, along with the open verdict, that we never really spoke about. I didn't know what he thought about it; I didn't know what he believed. I'd thought hard though. I had reached my conclusions and I knew what I believed. I didn't think the wave was my mum saying goodbye. I didn't think it was one last hug or a message from above telling me she was fine now, that she would always be watching over me or anything daft like that. I just don't believe in that kind of thing. I can't believe in that kind of thing. It was a coincidence and nothing more. But that doesn't make it any less special. It doesn't make it less important. The day we went to say goodbye to Mum, the day we finally laid her to rest, at that exact location, at that second of time, a wave as high as a house sprang from nowhere. It charged through our tiny spot of sea and flung us high into the air. And for a terrifying and glorious second we had no control over our lives and no say in what would happen next. And then we crash-landed, safe and slowly sound, and the wave rolled away to wherever waves roll to. It left us stunned and silent on a small yellow boat three miles out to sea. That's what happened, that's the truth. It was special. It was enough.

And I think that is enough.

Acknowledgements

Thank you Barry, Cynthia and Heather for love, support, patience and money.

And thank you to Julian Loose, Kate Murray-Browne and the team at Faber, Antony Harwood, Jelena Pasic-Peacock, James McGrath, Alex Bowden, Daniel Theobalds, Linda Le Cocq, Mark Ramsay and National Book Tokens.

Hello James Henry Ramsay.

ff

Faber and Faber – a home for writers

Faber and Faber is one of the great independent publishing houses in London. We were established in 1929 by Geoffrey Faber and our first editor was T. S. Eliot. We are proud to publish prize-winning fiction and non-fiction, as well as an unrivalled list of modern poets and playwrights. Among our list of writers we have five Booker Prize winners and eleven Nobel Laureates, and we continue to seek out the most exciting and innovative writers at work today.

www.faber.co.uk – a home for readers

The Faber website is a place where you will find all the latest news on our writers and events. You can listen to podcasts, preview new books, read specially commissioned articles and access reading guides, as well as entering competitions and enjoying a whole range of offers and exclusives. You can also browse the list of Faber Finds, an exciting new project where reader recommendations are helping to bring a wealth of lost classics back into print using the latest on-demand technology.